# QUEEN BITCH

# QUEEN BITCH

## THE KURTHERIAN GAMBIT™ BOOK 2

MICHAEL ANDERLE

DISRUPTIVE IMAGINATION®

This book is a work of fiction. All of the characters, organizations, and events portrayed in this novel are either products of the author's imagination or are used fictitiously. Sometimes both.

Copyright © 2021 Michael T. Anderle
Cover by Andrew Dobell, www.creativeedgestudios.co.uk
Cover copyright © LMBPN Publishing

LMBPN Publishing supports the right to free expression and the value of copyright. The purpose of copyright is to encourage writers and artists to produce the creative works that enrich our culture. The distribution of this book without permission is a theft of the author's intellectual property. If you would like permission to use material from the book (other than for review purposes), please contact support@lmbpn.com. Thank you for your support of the author's rights.

LMBPN Publishing
PMB 196, 2540 South Maryland Pkwy
Las Vegas, NV 89109

First US edition, 2015
Version 2.54, March 2021

The Kurtherian Gambit (and what happens within / characters / situations / worlds) are copyright © 2015-2021 by Michael T. Anderle.

QUEEN BITCH TEAM

**Thanks to the version 2.50 JIT Readers**

Jeff Eaton
Peter Manis
Dorothy Lloyd
Daniel Weigert
Diane L. Smith
Dave Hicks
Jackey Hankard-Brodie
Jeff Goode
Crystal Wren
Misty Roa
Shari Regan

*If I've missed anyone, please let me know!*

This version has been edited by the Skyhunter Editing Team.

DEDICATION

To Family, Friends and
Those Who Love
To Read.
May We All Enjoy Grace
To Live The Life We Are
Called.

# CHAPTER 1

**Brasov, Romania**

Bethany Anne waited for Ecaterina and Nathan to give her the most important information she needed to focus on for the next day.

Where could she go shopping?

In the last eight months, she had expected to die, been introduced to a vampire, been subjected to genetic changes to her body, and had to eat people.

Granted, for most of that time, she had been asleep. While she was sleeping, her alien symbiont was making changes to her body. But one had to admit the rest of it was pretty damn disturbing, and she was seriously in need of some shopping therapy. Especially a good pair of shoes. Well, maybe not. Since the changes to her body included making her legs six inches longer, maybe she didn't need the stiletto-heels short-girl workaround anymore.

She could hear Ecaterina, with her exotic and sexy Romanian accent, and Nathan talking. His good looks would officially be off the market if Ecaterina didn't screw up. He was drawn to her like a moth to a flame. She was just as interested in him, but her normal self-assurance had apparently been left behind. She constantly doubted herself and worried whether Nathan had any interest in her. Her self-doubt hid the obvious.

Not Bethany Anne's problem right now. She had a need to be dressed in anything but the ill-fitting rags she presently wore.

If you had asked most any man in Brasov—or the world, for that matter—Bethany Anne was a knockout. Black hair and a stellar, lithe body would have most guys working hard to not look at her. They would feel their wife's or girlfriend's eyes watching them like a hawk.

Both guys in the room with her right now had seen her when she wasn't at her best. Mind you, this wasn't a "bad hair day" kind of not her best, but rather a red eyes, fangs in her mouth, blood all over her face and hands as she killed supernatural wolves and drank their blood kind of not her best. It was a cockblocker for both Alexi and Nathan, as well it should be for any non-sociopathic male.

She had been helping both Alexi and Nathan overcome a serious difference of opinion with a local werewolf pack under the command of the late and certainly unlamented Algerian. He had received his marching orders from the vampire Petre, who made the mistake when trying to escape of paying attention to Ecaterina's spectacular cleavage instead of the bear trap that crushed his leg.

Hearing the screaming and a sudden thud, Bethany Anne had been worried about the spunky woman when she erupted out of the tunnel, only to find Petre laid out on the ground with his foot in the trap and Ecaterina buttoning up her shirt. That had made Bethany Anne's day.

In her present state of self-doubt, Ecaterina was worried Nathan—who was the most cautious Were in the world when it came to vampires—would succumb to Bethany Anne.

Ecaterina shouldn't have worried. A boyfriend was the last

thing on Bethany Anne's mind at that moment. She didn't have time for a boyfriend or even a friendly boy, for that matter.

Bethany Anne wanted a solid pair of Christian Louboutins in the worst way. She needed to feel like a woman for a while. Her abilities notwithstanding, she was accustomed to projecting confidence behind the armor of a Coach purse, a pair of Christian Louboutins, and a tailored suit, none of which should have bloodstains on them—something she couldn't say about most of the clothes she had worn for the past few days.

If they didn't hurry up and let her know what they'd found, she would start walking toward the center of town, and pity the person who interrupted her therapy efforts. It didn't help that she couldn't understand or read Romanian and Nathan had decided he needed to "brush up on his Romanian" around Ecaterina.

*Kiss-ass*, she thought.

Switching to English, Nathan got her attention and closed the laptop they had been using. "Okay, we think you should start at the Coresi Shopping Mall on the northeast side of town, and you can get yourself kitted out at the higher-end stores. From there, you will present a, uhh…" At this point, Nathan got the look on his face that suggested his sense of self-preservation had just kicked in. He ate whatever his next comment might have been and looked at Ecaterina, who had been standing behind him as he sat at the table.

Bethany Anne thought it was hilarious. According to Nathan, all the other vampires in the world were hardasses about comments that could be taken the wrong way. She didn't think she was that bad. Mind you, she still had a horrible temper, and she was known to have kicked a few guys' asses, or their twins, but she didn't have the predilection to immediately simply kill the offending person Nathan assumed she had because she was a vampire.

He was such a good-looking and dangerous man that she

couldn't get over how very circumspect he became around her at times. Fortunately, he had broken through this conditioning occasionally. Michael—her boss, in a way—had spent a thousand years making sure his strictures were followed on pain of death.

But Michael had disappeared. She wasn't sure if that was due to enemy action or prearranged intention on his part to leave her to clean up his mess. If it was the former, it was a pretty significant tell that she was in over her head by an enormous amount. He had a thousand years of experience and was the top badass in a group of badasses who made hardened military men feel the need to get religion. Dangerous men knew dangerous enemies.

This led her to conclude there was a very good chance he was still around. Where, she had no idea. She hoped and prayed he was trying to find out more about a serum that helped create intelligent Nosferatu. If the Forsaken, the splinter group of Michael's family that believed humans should be a subjugated race, truly had a workable serum, they could potentially create cannon fodder numbering in the billions for their army.

Since she knew nothing for sure, she couldn't accidentally give anything away.

She had been selected and changed to take the place of Bill, a vampire who had been killed in an ambush in Virginia a little less than a year ago. She knew getting back in contact with Bill's government liaison to see which, if any, operations needed her skills was a necessary step.

She also needed to talk to Stephen. He was one of Michael's immediate children and lived on the other side of the Carpathian Mountains. He was the parent of Petre, whom she had killed. She was, as a consequence, still shaking the dead vampire's imaginary dust out of her hair.

Nathan had wanted her to get permission before she took out Petre, but she decided introducing herself to the UnknownWorld in stricture-bending fashion was required to get the respect necessary to move forward with an agenda even Michael didn't know needed to occur.

Activities that included getting the world prepared for a possible intergalactic war in the not-so-distant future.

But before that happened, she was going to buy a nice pair of high heels.

### Washington DC, USA

The phone rang twice before Frank Kurns, the liaison between the UnknownWorld and the government, picked it up. "This is Frank." His rough voice, a little weak after almost a hundred years of living, wouldn't win any Tony awards.

He was in his office below ground under an old government building in Washington DC. It worked out well for him and those he might have to meet who wanted to remain anonymous or out of the sun. There were two old tunnels he could access from his level. One of them was left over from World War II, and the other he had built in the 70s. That one didn't show up on any plans for the building, historical or current.

The voice on the other end of the line was a mellow male baritone. "Good evening, Frank. It's Gerry." Gerry was the head of the American Pack Council and the Alpha of the New York pack, Nathan's direct Alpha.

"Good evening, Gerry. I've been expecting a call from you for the last few days. How can I help you?" Since Frank had asked a favor of Nathan, Gerry's second, a week and a half ago, he had expected to hear from Gerry when Nathan failed to contact him.

"I've got an update, if you can make heads or tails of it, and a concern."

"Let's hear both." Frank got comfortable in his chair.

"First, the update. Doesn't make a lot of sense to me, but my second sent me an email via a third party I'm not that familiar with. Says to let you know the lady was found, she was fully grown, and no dad in sight. I'm going out on a limb here and assuming this has to do with Michael?"

"Yes. Yes, it does. I suspect the fully-grown part means the woman is a vampire now. That isn't going to sit well with her dad necessarily, but the other option would be that she was dead. I'll have to find a way to make sure he at least knows she didn't die. Although I do wonder why your second didn't pass this on to me himself."

Gerry barked a little laugh. "Frank, you know Nathan. He's going to be pretty circumspect about anything he does around a vampire, even a young one who might not be all that strong. He would be concerned 'daddy' would show up. I'm not so sure she *is* weak, though. Nathan's one of the most careful guys in my pack. He must be with the vampire if he didn't call you directly. I imagine she doesn't want to talk to you yet."

"Then why did he get hold of you, and why isn't he concerned about updating you?"

"Well, I suspect she didn't absolutely forbid communicating with me. He has a responsibility to try to keep me in the loop, and through me, you. Why she isn't communicating with you would be my question. Do you know much about this new vamp?"

Frank considered his response. Right now, he needed any backing he could get. He had a lot of operations going pear-shaped because there wasn't an operative of Bill's caliber he could rely on. He had lost twenty-two men in seventeen raids, all of them black ops, because he hadn't had access to one of Michael's family to help him.

Since Michael and Carl had disappeared, he had no way to contact and coerce any of Michael's family to help. Michael ran the family in North America. There were some vampires in South America, but that was a Forsaken zone, and Frank never connected with them. They would certainly bite the hands that fed them. Well, the hands, the arms, the necks, and so on.

Frank answered Gerry's question. "Yes. Her name is Bethany Anne Reynolds, and she is—or was—an operative in a semi-black agency based here in Washington DC. I'm not sure I have all the particulars about how long it takes to convert someone to a vampire, but I didn't think it took more than a week, maybe two. Certainly not longer than a month, and she's been missing for over seven months. What did you mean earlier about not being so sure she's weak? I thought Michael took care of her conversion. That should just about guarantee she's pretty strong."

There was a pause on the line. Gerry finally spoke, drawing out his first word as he finished his thought. "Weeellll, that would make sense. Rumor has it the Brasov pack in Romania where Nathan went has suffered several highly placed members' deaths. Nathan didn't say he was in the hospital, and while *I* wouldn't want to take Nathan on, I feel pretty confident he didn't take out the seven Weres who are rumored to be dead right now. Oh, and one vampire."

"What?" Frank was astonished by this information. Given the right situation, Nathan Lowell could certainly have taken out seven pack members, as long as he didn't have to fight them all at once. Frank would bet against any one or two Weres taking Nathan down by themselves. But he highly doubted Nathan killed seven Weres and a vampire. One, his task hadn't been to get involved, merely to locate and report his findings. Two, Frank couldn't imagine what could happen that might cause Nathan to get involved beyond Frank's find-and-report request. It wasn't like there was anyone there he cared about, and Frank doubted Nathan would ignore his sense of self-preservation to fall for Bethany Anne, as pretty as she was.

"Yeah. European Council has been hearing about some shady connections between the Brasov pack Alpha Algerian, and Petre, one of Stephen's kids. Now, the Council was contacted by someone from the pack in Brasov about midway down in the hierarchy. Seems someone cleaned out half the pack, starting at the top. When this person went to get information from Petre, his house had been trashed in a fire and had two burnt bodies inside. One of them had an arm and, get this, a head missing. They found the burnt skull on the other side of the room. These two bodies were the Were officers who hung with Petre for daytime protection. They were able to locate Petre's exits, and found one that opened up about two hundred yards away. There was a bloody bear trap sprung by the hole. They could still smell a little of Petre's blood on the trap, but no Petre."

Frank's mind tried furiously to work out the ramifications of everything Gerry told him. He needed to get more information, and Frank's advisor was most likely not permitted to contact him now. Wonderful.

"Damn, Gerry. Now that you've given me more than a headache, I'm afraid to ask what your concerns might be. Want to share them with me?"

Frank heard Gerry sigh. "Yeah. It's the young and dumb. They haven't seen a really scary vampire in years, and now they're starting to act up. The Council can put a lid on it for just so long before either a vampire needs to take care of it, or the Council will have to decide which way they really want to go with this 'not telling the world' stricture. When we had Michael to lay the blame on, it was easy to just say it wasn't in our power to deal with. Now Michael's gone missing, or at least, that's the rumor…"

Frank knew Gerry wanted information, so he sighed and confirmed Gerry's unasked question. "Yes, Michael is missing. As I said, Nathan was supposed to find and report on Michael and Bethany Anne. Apparently, he's found Bethany Anne, and God only knows what else he's been up to. Except for giving me an update, of course."

"He did, just not to your face. You tell me the next time *you* want to ignore a vampire, and I'll get ready for your funeral."

"Okay, good point. So you guys want what from me, exactly?"

"I need to get Nathan's input and your thoughts. What do you think will happen if we allow more werewolf sightings to occur?"

Gerry knew very well what would happen, Frank thought. It wouldn't be a pretty situation at all. If humans could confirm the existence of the supernatural, all sorts of problems would arise. He could think of a few that would be pretty negative, and that didn't even include what the major religions would say.

Frank really wished Michael would show up. He hadn't appreciated how quiet everything was when the dreaded vampire patriarch was around to enforce his rulings. There must be a lot of pent-up aggression just waiting to pop if anyone could confirm Michael was dead.

He needed to get in contact with Bethany Anne.

"Let me see if I can get in touch with Bethany Anne. I'm not sure what she can do to scare the young and dumb, as you put it, but she *is* a vampire and will probably talk to me. The rest of Michael's kids only talk to Carl, and he's missing as well. If it goes completely in the can, I can see about contacting her dad. God, this is a mess."

Frank heard Gerry sigh again over the phone. "Yeah. If and when you talk to Nathan, let him know I need him back here in the States. He's got a bit of a reputation for not taking shit from anyone, so maybe he can be the boogeyman for a while."

"All right, let me see what assets I have in Romania who might be able to find them. Talk to you later, Gerry."

"Take care, Frank. Let me know if you hear anything. Bye."

Frank put his handset down and rubbed his face in frustration. Not only did he need help with the mayhem and destruction, but now the Weres were getting involved and causing friction. This whole pot would explode if someone didn't put a lid back on it, and quickly.

CHAPTER 2

**Zurich, Switzerland**

Bethany Anne felt pretty good. She had been able to find two sets of clothes to mix and match in Brasov, and then in Zurich, she was able to pick up an additional two outfits and another pair of shoes. The train ride over there hadn't been too bad either. She was still taking in Etheric energy, and TOM said she could probably pull off two translocations before needing to "hit the vein," as he called it. She had stayed in her sleeper compartment for the duration of the trip, resting up, and had let Nathan know he would need to give her a heads-up if he felt they were in danger.

Ecaterina had stayed behind in Brasov to take care of a few things. They would meet up in a couple of days, before Bethany Anne went to wake Stephen up—assuming no one else woke him and told him about Petre's demise.

While they had been in the shopping mall in Brasov, Nathan had recognized the perfume and then the face of a woman who had tracked him and bugged his clothes when he'd first gotten to Brasov. She was pretty hesitant when he approached her. Bethany Anne kept half an eye on the situation while she tried on one of three pairs of shoes she liked.

## QUEEN BITCH

The two of them stepped out into the courtyard to talk. Bethany Anne noticed Nathan looking around discreetly to see who else could be watching them.

Bethany Anne decided to pay for the pair that suited and ask the clerk to hold them. Fortunately, the lady's English was good enough to understand her.

Alexi, Ecaterina's werebear uncle, was visiting family before going home to live on his mountain. Bethany Anne knew where to find him should she need him and besides, Alexi wasn't one who enjoyed company.

Ecaterina had decided to come with Bethany Anne to the States, as expected. She was currently with her brother Ivan, getting some business taken care of and setting up the discussion to tell their parents she was leaving. Well, leaving with a man who was unmarried and a woman they didn't know. She wasn't concerned about her dad, but she said her mom would have, "how you say, a bunch of cows?" It was kittens, but Bethany Anne wasn't going to correct everything she got wrong. Idiomatic English was something best experienced.

Bethany Anne found it hilarious when Ecaterina didn't give any of Nathan's money back for the trip he had contracted with her. She said it was to make sure that Ivan learned it didn't matter "how nice a man is, or good looking." She had earned her pay, and then some. Ivan should learn from her example and make sure the cute women didn't take him for more money. Especially now that she wasn't going to be there to protect him from the dimples.

The pretty woman the Were was talking to left. Bethany Anne raised an eyebrow and looked inquisitively at Nathan as they followed her from the store.

"Local pack representative. They've tracked their problems back to me and 'forces unknown.' They didn't agree with how Algerian was getting them involved with Petre, and now that everyone who was pro-vampire is dead, they wanted to make sure I wasn't gunning for them." He smiled, and his face lit up. "One problem taken care of!"

Bethany Anne watched the woman walk across the courtyard. Just before she got to the other side, about thirty yards away, two men joined her, and they all walked around the corner.

"How can we be sure they're telling the truth?"

Nathan glanced over to where Bethany Anne was looking. "Pack politics. She says it wasn't just the Brasov pack that wanted the situation stopped, but that the pack contacted the EPC and got a directive from the Council. Without Algerian here, they don't have any way to argue the ruling should they want to. I can't call Gerry in the States and ask him to confirm the ruling."

Bethany Anne looked back at Nathan. "You can't call?"

He shook his head. "No. Well, I could, but it would be breaking a few rules of decorum around here. If someone from Europe did the same thing in America, it wouldn't raise too many eyebrows. Here in Europe, they'd get their boxers in a twist if I did it." He watched Bethany Anne's eyebrows start to draw together.

"Is that sooo?"

Nathan was by now accustomed to Bethany Anne's careless disregard for proper channels of communication. He wouldn't be too surprised if she decided to make the call herself, and he resigned himself to whatever she wanted to do. It wasn't as if he would be able to change her mind anyway.

---

Bethany Anne in a fashionable dark-gray suit and Nathan in a casual sports coat over jeans entered the Swiss bank. It was a monument to the use of stone as a building material. The beautiful entryway towered over forty feet, and their shoes clicked and clacked over the stone floor that had to have been in place for centuries.

QUEEN BITCH

Two security guards flanked the entrance into the main banking area. A row of tellers lined the left side, a group of cubicle offices were on the right, and four couches had been placed in a square on a carpet in the middle as a waiting area. A receptionist sat at a desk in front of the waiting area. Large televisions in all the corners were tuned to finance stations. Only one showed CNN.

The two of them walked over to the desk, and the lady was quick to smile at them. Bethany Anne chuckled when she took a little longer to greet Nathan. His easy smile and warm handshake seemed to sweep her off her feet.

Bethany Anne rolled her eyes. "Excuse me?"

The receptionist quickly looked at Bethany Anne, blushing faintly. "Yes, madam, how can we help you?"

"I have had accounts opened for me, and I require access to those accounts and an explanation of the details of them. Who can help me with this?"

The receptionist looked down at her phone, different lines blinking on and off. "You would need to speak to Mr. Berger. Unfortunately, he's on the phone at the moment. May I get your name and let him know you are waiting?"

"My name is Bethany Anne. Please let him know I am not terribly patient."

The receptionist took her information coolly and picked up the phone to make a call. Bethany Anne and Nathan went around the desk to sit on a couch.

Nathan spoke in a low voice so it wouldn't carry very far. "Why didn't you give your last name? Will he be able to find you?"

Bethany Anne took a breath and looked at Nathan. "Oh, yes, he'll know who I am. This bank does business with vampires. I can smell their scent. Faint, but it's there. Plus, vampires don't have last names, Mr. Lowell. I gave up Reynolds when I changed, at least for the foreseeable future. You know how you've had to

13

deal with money issues because you live so long? Well, compound that by ten. Michael set up a group in this bank and a couple of ancillaries to handle the situation without having to create new personas every thirty years or so. If Mr. Berger isn't part of the 'in' group, I imagine my name will be flagged and we'll get a different contact."

"How will you know if he knows anything?"

Bethany Anne smiled at Nathan. "Why, Mr. Lowell, I'll see him sweat."

---

Kevin Berger was having a fine day. He had just gotten off the phone with a small business that had decided to move their accounts to his bank. While not something that would get him a raise, with enough of these little victories he would be on track to receive a great quarterly review.

His message-waiting light was on, so he picked up the phone and called the receptionist. She explained that an "impatient American" was waiting for him in the lobby. He got the American lady's name and hung up.

Not even an impatient American would ruin the triumph he felt right now. He ran the name through the system to see if anything was pending for her.

Not only was something pending, but there was also a flag next to her name. The blood drained from his face. Here was a way to ruin his feel-good moment.

He opened the necessary files and reviewed them. This… lady…was to have access to eight accounts. He quickly hit the keys to review the accounts, and had there been any blood left in his face to drain, it would have done so now.

There was enough money in these accounts to float a small-to-medium nation. Not only was she Nacht, but she also had to be high up to access this kind of money. He literally couldn't afford to upset her, or his quarterly review would be unnecessary. He would either be out of a job, or possibly—if he upset her enough— he would hope for a quick death.

Kevin was on the inside, as it was called in the bank, but this was his first meeting with a real Nacht. Since he worked days only, he had never considered he would be called on to interact with any of them.

He quickly grabbed all the paperwork he would need, stuffed it into folders, and closed and locked his computer. There was only one way Nacht were allowed to confirm their…uniqueness. He really hoped she wasn't hungry.

Putting on his coat—and hopefully hiding the perspiration under his arms—he went out to meet his newest client. Unfortunately, the receptionist had it all wrong. Everything he knew about Nacht suggested to him this lady was being incredibly patient. He tried not to jog out onto the floor.

CHAPTER 3

**Zurich, Switzerland**
Nathan looked around the bank, but mostly watched the large television that had CNN running. He heard quick footsteps approaching, so he pivoted his head to find out what was happening. He didn't expect anything bad, but he wasn't a fool, either.

A younger man, probably mid-thirties, in a three-piece darkblue suit with red pinstripes headed in their direction at the fastest pace he could without jogging. Nathan realized this man must be "in the know." He was sweating, and his eyes kept shifting to Bethany Anne and away again.

Nathan watched as the receptionist realized the director was stressed and slid her hand under her desk. The guy saw this and surreptitiously shook his head, and the receptionist removed her hand.

Beside him, Bethany Anne stood up. If he could get past the vampire thing, she was an incredibly beautiful woman. Her gracefulness led one to believe she must have been a ballerina. Her looks even caused the bank representative to do a double-take. It was obvious the person he'd expected to meet and the person he actually was meeting didn't coincide.

"Ms. Bethany Anne? I'm Kevin Berger, your representative, and I can help complete your accounts', um, set-up so you may access the funds. Would you walk with me?"

Bethany Anne took his hand graciously and shook it. "Certainly, Mr. Berger. Please lead on. My compatriot Mr. Lowell will be joining us." She didn't ask for Mr. Berger's permission for Nathan to come, but he wasn't about to refuse this woman anything.

He led the way across the foyer and went to a wall clad in wood. He pushed a small catch which was hard to see that opened a door. When it was open, he stood aside. Nathan went in first, followed by Bethany Anne, who smiled sweetly at Berger.

He gulped and closed the door behind them.

Inside was a short hallway with a coffee bar, refrigerator, and snacks all laid out on the left, and on the right, in a room about twelve by fifteen feet, was a couch on the near wall with a gorgeous rug and a coffee table. Toward the other end was a table with three chairs around it. When the door shut behind them, you could feel the pressure. This room was soundproof.

"Would either of you care for refreshments?" He hoped he wasn't merely supposed to offer his neck. Kevin grimaced. He was glad they didn't see him roll his eyes at his own stupidity.

"No, we're both good, Mr. Berger."

"Very good, Ms. Bethany Anne. Would you care to join me at the table? This is a soundproof room, and there are no electronic recording devices allowed. I have the bank's full confidence. Since the Nacht set up the requirements for verification, nothing is allowed to be recorded."

Bethany Anne looked at Nathan. He took out a small box from his jacket and retrieved a little rectangular device that he plugged into his phone. In a minute, he shook his head at Bethany Anne.

"Very good, Mr. Berger. How do you want me to confirm, or verify, my identity?"

"You don't know?" Kevin wanted to slap himself. His surprise that the lady in front of him didn't already know the method of verification had slipped past his mouth at a most inopportune time.

"No, Mr. Berger. Would you care to enlighten me, or do I have to play twenty questions? I can guarantee that after the first two I will get very annoyed."

Bethany Anne was getting a little worried. She'd thought she'd simply have to give some DNA or something. That was what Carl had expected. Maybe he didn't understand the true method?

The sweat beaded on Kevin's forehead. "Um, my lady, you don't have to prove *who* you are. Rather, you have to verify that you are, in fact, a vampire."

Bethany Anne wanted to laugh out loud. The bank representative went from concerned to deathly afraid in a second when he had to say "vampire" out loud.

Did every person think the only thing vampires did was drink blood? While it was tempting to see what he would do if she did bring her fangs out, she decided she might try other ideas first.

"Mr. Berger, are there specified ways to prove my unnaturalness? I presume you don't want me to bite you, right?" She had a difficult time not smacking her lips while glancing at his neck. She didn't really need to smell him urinate right here.

"Well, to be honest, it wasn't ever expected that I would have to actually perform one of these introductions. I, uh, I believe merely showing me your fangs might work?"

He sounded so hopeful that she almost did as he asked. However, she could think of a few ways a non-vampire could try to trick someone. She needed him for future work and didn't want him ignorant.

"How about we do this, Mr. Berger? I will slap your head off your shoulders. If I fail, then you know for sure I am not a vampire. However, if I succeed… No, I guess that will just make a significant mess."

Kevin was rapidly nodding at this point.

Seriously? Bethany Anne was almost pissed she had to do something as prosaic as showing her fangs. She wanted to do something classy. It was then that Nathan cocked his head and turned it toward the entrance.

Bethany Anne heard the noise as well. It seemed the bank was being robbed.

In a calm yet annoyed voice, Bethany Anne spoke. "Those fucktards are messing up my day. I swear to God, if I get any blood on my suit, I will shove their guns up their asses." She assumed anything she did that might show up on video would be erased before anyone could see it. What was the worst that could happen, Michael would show up to spank her? If only he *would* show up, so she could give him a piece of her mind.

She took off her pumps and set them on the table, walked toward the door, and disappeared.

Kevin's mouth dropped open and he looked at Nathan, who was still staring toward the door. It was soundproof, so what was he listening to?

Kevin started for the door.

Nathan put out his arm to stop him. "You need to go back to where you were standing a minute ago. She'll be right back, and if she doesn't come through the door, you don't want to be where she might end up. I'm absolutely sure it would ruin your day."

Kevin stepped back into his original space. She reappeared, but this time with two pistols and an AR-15. She handed the rifle and one of the pistols to Nathan and slid one into her waistband. She looked over her shoulder. "Remind me to get a shoulder holster, would you, Nathan?"

Nathan nodded, checked out the AR-15, and put the safety on both guns before moving to the hallway. He faced it as if he expected that someone might come in.

Bethany Anne caught Kevin's attention. "Sorry about that. Your bank was being robbed. I would really hate to have my day interrupted."

"What…what did you do?" Kevin's face had gone white when he saw the guns the lady suddenly appeared with.

"Hmmm? Oh, I just took the guns away from the annoying fuck-nuts outside who wanted to rob your bank. I don't have time to deal with the cops right now. Can we get moving with this? Does disappearing and reappearing with guns suit you as verification? If not, I could use a little energy." When she finished saying that, she willed her eyes to start moving into the red realm on purpose. Usually, they went red when she was completely vamping out, but she'd had a discussion with TOM, and he had explained he could manipulate the right nerves to get the effect.

It succeeded splendidly. "No, no, translocation works for me. I have the documents and the account numbers right here for you." He quickly sat down at the table and pulled out the documents and a pen from inside his jacket. He directed her to all the locations where she needed to sign and provided copies for her.

Bethany Anne finished all the signatures, took the copies, and slipped the envelope into her Coach purse.

There was a knock at the door, and Nathan raised an eyebrow at Bethany Anne, who turned to Kevin. "Mr. Berger, I really don't want to be interrupted right now. Please see what they want. Oh, and I'll need appropriate credit cards to pull from my accounts. How do I go about procuring three sets of cards?"

The knock was repeated. Kevin jumped up and slipped by Nathan to crack the door an inch and talk to a person on the other side. He closed the door quickly and came back into the room. "As you said, there was a robbery attempt, and the police are interviewing everyone before they leave the building. I explained that you were a very important client who didn't want to be involved, but they are very confused about what happened outside. One minute the criminals had guns and black masks, and the next they were all on the floor without their masks or guns. They have them all cuffed but don't understand what happened. They are asking for our video."

"Who did you talk to out there?"

"A local officer, I think. I'm sure an inspector will be here as soon as he can."

"When the Inspector arrives, please have him come in here. I'll take care of his questions. I'll need a large hat and veil to get back out of here."

"Why wouldn't you just…" Kevin moved his hands around as if something exploded.

"I would have to request a small token of your affection, Mr. Berger. Say, a few ounces. Are you offering?"

"No, no. I am sorry for letting my curiosity go like that. It was inexcusable. I will find a hat, my lady." With that, Kevin bowed and went out the door.

Nathan sat on the couch, out of the direct line of sight of someone coming in the door. "So that disappearing trick takes a bunch of energy?"

"Always trying to get information, aren't we, Nathan?" Bethany Anne smiled mischievously. "But I didn't use much energy for what I did. I just wanted to encourage Mr. Berger here to be a little more circumspect."

"Can you take someone with you?"

Bethany Anne pursed her lips. "I don't know. If I do, it might take a dramatically larger amount of energy. I could end up on the other side immediately needing a top up, and the person I took might become my snack. Seems a little risky."

"Do you always have to, ah, eat them?" Nathan was thinking back to the clearing where they had first met. Bethany Anne had plucked at least eighty pounds of hungry wolf out of the air as if it were a feather. Then, she'd proceeded to rip its neck open and drink before dropping the lifeless body on the ground in front of him. It had made a very deep impression.

"You know, Nathan, I really haven't tried just taking a little sip yet. How about we try it real quick?"

Nathan suddenly realized how the presently missing Mr. Berger felt. It was a damn useful way to shut someone up quickly.

"I'm good, thanks."

A few minutes later, there was a knock on the door, and Mr. Berger came back in. He handed Bethany Anne a small manila envelope. "My lady, here are the cards that allow you access to the accounts at any cash access point almost anywhere in Europe. The inspector is here and will be coming this way shortly. I've made sure the video will not be available. As someone with responsibility for your accounts, I have the ability to override even the bank's president if necessary. We will give them any video that doesn't directly show what happened. They will be less than pleased, but they don't have a bank robbery to solve either. I think they came out ahead on this one. Finally, I have a lady out purchasing the requested hat and veil right now."

"Very good, Mr. Berger. While I wait, would you give me a printout of the accounts and any annuities and how the income is derived and how much is in cash? Thank you so much." Kevin bowed his head and left.

"What do you want to do with the weapons?" Nathan looked longingly at the AR-15.

"Well, we can probably get away with the pistols, but I'm not sure how to deal with the rifle. It isn't like we can take it with us on the train. Then again, I suppose we could get a case to hide it in."

"It's not traceable to us, and I'd feel a little better with a couple of weapons. The randomness of this attack concerns me."

"Why, you don't think it's random?" Bethany Anne went over to the couch and sat down. Nathan stuck the pistol in his waistband under his coat. Setting the rifle down beside the couch, he joined Bethany Anne.

"Yes, I think it *was* most likely random. To assume every

problem is an enemy action targeted at you just leads to crazy, but to not take precautions in case I'm wrong and it *is* enemy action is also foolish. Just because the EPC told the Brasov pack to back down doesn't mean there isn't a suborning team on the Council that wouldn't like to take out a new vamp."

Bethany Anne raised an eyebrow at Nathan.

"Look, everyone pretty much assumes new vamps aren't as powerful as you are."

"One minute." Bethany Anne went inside herself for a moment.

*TOM, what's the story behind this "weak vampire" comment?*

**It makes sense, Bethany Anne. When you consider that the nanocytes are propagating and giving some of the best and worst features of the donor to their next host, they won't be as pure as those from my ship. With each generation, it will take longer to accomplish the change, and the connections to the Etheric would take time as well. There would be fewer nanocytes created capable of connecting to the Etheric. However, not even Michael has as many nanocytes as you, and I stay on top of what they are doing at all times. Michael was never taught how to direct the efforts, so I doubt any of the other children know it can be done either.**

*That's interesting. I didn't know this.*

**You have me.**

*Right, but not forever. Don't forget I expect to eventually find a way to provide you with a different host to annoy.*

**You wound me, Bethany Anne. I've been quiet for a while.**

*I know, and it worries me.*

**Why?**

*As with a small child, the biggest problems happen when they are quietest. When we get done here, you and I are going to talk.*

Bethany Anne didn't get a response, which confirmed her suspicion that TOM was up to something and didn't want to own up to it. Damn. Served her right for ignoring him for the last week. She turned back to Nathan. "Okay, what you're saying makes complete sense. It's very unlikely a regular vampire would be as powerful as I am."

It was Nathan's turn to ponder in silence for a minute. "So, this could have been set up to see how you reacted?" There was a knock on the door. Nathan stood up and motioned for Bethany Anne to stay seated. She hid a smile at how this man took responsibility for protection despite his objective experience that she was better-suited to handle problems than even he was. However, he certainly caused more people to reconsider violence when they took a look at him.

Nathan came back after closing the door and offered her a shopping bag with a large box inside. Bethany Anne pulled the box out and set it on the coffee table. It contained a very fashionable hat with a black veil, which would keep any cameras from getting a good picture of her face.

Nathan snorted, and she giggled like a little girl trying on the hat. "How do I look?"

He shook his head but was saved from having to answer that question by another knock on the door. He went to it and looked out. Seeing the inspector, he opened the door and allowed him in.

## CHAPTER 4

**Zurich, Switzerland**

If Inspector Golay hadn't been directed to this section of the wood-covered wall, he wouldn't have realized there was a door there.

Whoever was inside must be important to the bank. They didn't want to be part of the circus out here. While he could sympathize, he wasn't willing to treat anyone as special simply because the bank's management would wring their hands.

He was still annoyed at the video runaround. To have it all be available except for the clips where the criminals were taken down was beyond suspect. It was a crime to keep evidence out of the hands of the police.

This bank was one of Switzerland's oldest, and they had secrets from their secrets. Trying to get too much information out of them would certainly bring him headaches—if not from his chief, then from people leaning on his chief.

The rumor was that it was a couple of Americans. While it was not particularly rare for Americans to bank in Switzerland, avoiding publicity was not what you expected. They usually seemed to be publicity hounds.

The door opened and one of the biggest men Inspector Golay had ever seen stood in front of him. He was dressed in a sports jacket and had a couple of days' growth on his cheeks. He glanced behind the Inspector and opened the door to let him in.

This man was a professional. Right now, he was a professional guard, it seemed, but he wasn't so sure the man wasn't a professional in the darker deeds, as well.

When he stepped into the suite, the door shut behind him, and all noise ceased. Ah, he thought, soundproof.

He pulled out his recorder as he walked farther into the room. To his left, a lady in a suit, hat, and veil sat demurely on the couch.

"Welcome, Inspector. How can we help you today?"

"Thank you, I appreciate your willingness to talk to me. Do you mind taking the hat off?"

"Why would you need me to do that, Inspector?" He could see enough of her lower face to see a small smile.

He looked around, walked over to the table, grabbed a chair, brought it back to the couch, and sat down. "I like to see the eyes of the people I speak with. Certainly, you have nothing to hide?" She smiled at him but said nothing and didn't take the hat off.

"Inspector, are you suggesting an American woman was able to take down those bank robbers and no one was able to see?" She lifted a foot and a very shapely leg from behind the coffee table. "In high heels, no less? This is what I'm trying to hide?"

Well, it was obvious she hadn't gone out in those high heels and taken down alert bank robbers. Even in the conservative suit, he was sure no man would fail to notice her.

He looked up at the guard, who had come to stand by the couch, his arms crossed in front of him. "What about you?" He looked down at his notes. He had stopped by the receptionist's desk and written down the names of all the people who had waited in line for help. "Mr. Lowell?"

The man's green eyes stared back at the Inspector, completely at ease with him knowing his name. "I'm sorry, Inspector. I haven't been out of the room since we came in. I didn't see anything out in the teller area, and I can't help. I wish I could." He shrugged.

The Inspector knew he was both getting the runaround and wasting his time. They had good alibis. People had seen them coming into the room but not leaving. The door had never opened. He felt sure someone would have noticed if a door had unexpectedly appeared in the wall.

But something nagged at him. They were too calm, too collected. They should be talking about it, at least.

He looked around the room, keeping them in his peripheral vision. "Did you know the robbers' guns disappeared?"

Ah! He got a little start from the man, who had looked down at the lady. Maybe this wouldn't be a waste of his time.

Bethany Anne decided to take control of the conversation. "Why, yes, Inspector Golay. I did know. How do you believe it occurred?" What had Ecaterina said back with Petre? Oh yes, "Father said to use the right bait." She stood up and walked right by the Inspector on her way to the table, which allowed Nathan to sit on the couch where she had been. The Inspector's eyes followed Bethany Anne the whole way, ignoring the Were.

Nathan took the time to push the AR-15 farther under the couch, hiding it well unless the Inspector chose to get on his hands and knees to look.

"Well, I don't really know. That is why I am asking you. I thought perhaps Americans would know better? There seem to be guns all over the United States."

Bethany Anne started laughing quietly. To think that *she* was thrown into the "gun-toting American" stereotype. If the Inspector knew how dangerous she could be without a gun, he wouldn't have worried about asking her that question. Then she realized it wasn't a stereotype. Both she and Nathan had guns on them at that very moment. They hadn't brought them into the bank, but they *did* have them and planned on keeping them. *Gott Verdammt*, his profile was right in this case. Bethany Anne hated being a stereotype. She sighed and faced him, raising her arms just a little to accentuate her figure. "Do you need to search me, Inspector?"

Inspector Golay started sweating. This woman had just turned the tables on him. She was playing with him. He was tempted to inspect her simply to be a prick. Still, neither had an AR-15 under their coat. She wasn't hiding anything illegal—possibly immoral, but not illegal—under her suit coat. He stood up. "Certainly not, *Fräulein*. I appreciate your time, and should I have any additional questions, where might I contact you?"

"I'm sorry, Inspector, Mr. Lowell and I are only here to take care of banking business. We'll be leaving in a couple of hours."

"Are you heading back to America, *Fräulein*?"

"No, we're actually heading back to Romania, Inspector. May we go now?"

"Certainly. I will see myself out and let the others know you may leave. Have a pleasant day."

With that, Inspector Golay tipped his head at Nathan and left the two Americans in the room.

---

On the train, Nathan spotted two men who were surreptitiously paying attention to Bethany Anne. Each had taken a seat which allowed him to see the door to her sleeping compartment. One, Nathan had pegged as probably merely someone who was excited by her looks. The other, however, had an edge that suggested a hunter. Probably a government agent.

He knocked on Bethany Anne's door. "Yes?"

"It's Nathan. Do you have a moment?" She cracked the door and peeked through the slit, raising an eyebrow.

"Privately?" She pursed her lips and opened the door to let

him in. The sleeping compartment was very small. She liked to lie down and hadn't wanted to share a compartment, so she had purchased her own and asked Nathan what he wanted. He wasn't sleepy and had opted to sit in a seat in the car to see what was going on. He still wasn't comfortable about the robbery happening while they were at the bank.

She wore a nightgown and a robe. Appropriate, but hardly demure. Fortunately, he was still well aware of her dark side and frankly, he was anxious to see Ecaterina again. Ecaterina was gorgeous, fun, gregarious, enjoyed the outdoors, and didn't have red eyes. A major plus for Nathan. Plus, she had an accent to die for. He had almost died for Ecaterina once already.

Nathan got to the point. "We have two guys watching your compartment. I think one has a romantic interest, but the other is probably undercover."

"You mean like an inspector from the police at the bank?"

"No, like a government individual."

"European?"

"Could be, or he might be American. I can't tell, and I haven't talked to him yet. I haven't spoken to Frank in a while, so he could be someone sent to look after me looking after you. Or it could be pack-related. Either way, I've been out of touch."

Bethany Anne felt a pang of remorse. She knew she had taken too much of Nathan's time, but she was new to the Unknown-World and needed him as a lifeline to keep her from screwing up too badly. But she also shouldn't take advantage of her admittedly few friends right now.

"I guess we do need to talk to Frank, but I refuse to label it 'checking in.' I'm not a big fan of someone thinking he has me on the proverbial leash. You either." Then she smiled up at Nathan in that "I'm going to have fun at your expense" way he was getting used to. "Well, let's be honest, I'm only okay with holding your leash myself, or maybe Ecaterina?"

Big bad Mr. Lowell looked down at the shorter vampire, and

he both blushed and gave her a long-suffering look. "That obvious?"

"Only to everyone, Nathan. You know she has it bad for you too, right?" Bethany Anne hadn't promised to not get involved, and the longer these two danced around each other, the more annoying it was.

"Really?"

Bethany Anne rolled her eyes. "It's obvious to Alexi, Ivan, and me. The only two clueless ones are you and Ecaterina. You're like two teenagers mooning over each other. Wipe that grin off your face, Nathan. What do you suggest we do about you checking with your Council and Frank and our unexpected guests outside?"

Nathan tried to dampen his smile and focus on her questions, but Bethany Anne shouldn't have confirmed Ecaterina liked him if she wanted his full attention.

"Ah, damn. Uhhhh, let me call Gerry and get the lay of the land, and then I'll talk to Frank. Do you want to talk to either of them?"

"Not yet. I don't mind you updating Frank about what's going on, but I don't want him to think I need anything from him right now. Hell, maybe never, considering what was in the accounts."

Yeah, that was true, thought Nathan. When Bethany Anne had shared she was officially independently wealthy, he was simultaneously relieved and concerned. If Michael had given her access to that much wealth, it could lead one to believe that he wasn't expecting to be around for a while, if ever. She had access to all of Michael's holdings all over the world. She had asked him to keep the particulars to himself but that he should share his suppositions and concerns regarding Michael with her.

"Nathan, once you talk to Gerry and Frank, I think we need to make further plans. I'll understand if you need to go back to the States. Ecaterina and I will follow you as soon as I finish with

Stephen. I value everything you've done for me, and I hope we can stay friends?"

Nathan was surprised. Bethany Anne had been very aloof since they had met. This was the first time she had offered him the hand of friendship. "So, if I ask again how you got back up with a hole in your stomach I could see the wall through, you'll tell me?" He smiled at the memory.

Bethany Anne smiled back, "Yeah, okay." She put her fingers really close together. "Maybe only one minute away, Mr. Lowell."

She started getting out a pair of jeans and a shirt. "Give me a couple of minutes to get dressed, and you can use my compartment. Check the compartment for bugs before you call. I'll go hit the restroom and get a bite to eat."

Nathan smiled and stepped out of the compartment.

---

Bethany Anne set her hat on her head and opened the door. Nathan stood from a seat a few feet away. She stepped out and let him go into her sleeping compartment to talk to Gerry and Frank.

She walked toward the bar/buffet car. With her Premier ticket, the food was included. She hadn't any previous experience with eating on a train and enjoyed the prospect. Everything looked pretty posh to her.

The seats were upholstered in a deep-red velvet, the tables had white linens, and red drapes covered the windows. There was a huge amount of polished brass in the car. It was certainly an upscale experience. She sat down at a table with two places. She didn't want to be rude and take a whole booth for herself, and wasn't sure how long Nathan would be on the phone. She had been pretty strict about not allowing him to check in, and now she had to suffer the consequences. The calls were likely to be long.

When the waiter came over and inquired what kind of wine she might like, she smiled and asked him to surprise her. With her hat on, an affectation she had to admit she enjoyed, all people could see were her mouth and chin. She just watched the countryside slide by for a moment.

She had a lot to accomplish, and Michael had afforded her the means to do anything she wanted. She had the money and accumulated wealth a thousand years had brought, and frankly, she was overwhelmed.

She thought back to the basics. Shelter, water, and food. Well, she didn't suffer from a lack of shelter if she trusted Michael's homes across the world. Leafing through the documents, she had found multiple domiciles on all the major continents and a few very secret places in South America and Africa. She guessed that made sense with his Forsaken children in that area.

But did she want to use them?

Her wine came, and she thanked the waiter and took a sip. A very nice Chianti Classico from Italy, she had been told. It *was* nice. She noticed a black rooster design on the neck of the bottle before he took off the seal.

She was still trying to understand her life. She needed to consider short-term goals, such as talking with Stephen and connecting with the UnknownWorld, while still planning for the distant future when the world would need to be able to defend itself.

*TOM, what do we need to produce the parts for our ship?*

*Our ship?*

*You keep calling this our body. It makes sense to me.*

She sensed TOM was a bit befuddled. Ever since the organic computer had been placed in her head, she had been connecting better with TOM.

**Okay. I guess that makes sense, but it is a bit much to understand. I'm in your body, so we *are* sharing it. The ship**

was mine, but I can't take control of it back without a body, so I guess you're right.

*Back to the question, TOM.*

Well, it needs two structural joints that were destroyed when landing. Without them, we can't get the landing legs to retract into the body, and the craft would not work without atmosphere. Other than that, the whole body will need surveying and patching with some rather sophisticated alloys I'm not sure your world has available yet, and of course, there is the jump-engine, and anything else that might have been affected when I came in on the last jump. I didn't have time to do a full diagnostic on the engine, and you can't do one in atmosphere.

*So, to summarize, with the landing gear fixed we could go out of the atmosphere. But what about here on the ground? Why didn't you ever move the ship after you landed?*

I'm not sure what other pieces were broken, and while it had power, I didn't want to chance destroying it completely with another ascent and descent. When Michael came to the ship within thirty or forty solar turns, I believed I was in a good enough place. I didn't realize I wouldn't see anyone else until your arrival.

Bethany Anne considered his statement. The ship was probably capable of making a trip to a hangar she could acquire. There, they would look into refurbishment and reverse engineering. But how would she accomplish this without getting the tinfoil-hat groups or governments involved? She knew her own government would grab the ship and stuff it into a black hole even *she* would have trouble getting it out of. It spoke to why powerful people worked with smaller and more easily manipulated governments.

But if she were going to make a difference, she would eventually have to work with the major powers. All of them—the US, China, Russia, India, and the Europeans. If she decided to start with a smaller country it would make it harder for any of the big governments to get involved, but not impossible. Plus, she doubted that even with as much pull as she might now have, she had more than the biggest governments.

What a freaking headache. She finished her glass of wine.

"Would the beautiful lady allow me to provide her second glass of wine?"

Bethany Anne looked through the veil to see a spectacular example of a well-groomed and cultured European gentleman in front of her. With dark hair, an Italian suit and shoes, gold cufflinks, and a glass of wine in each hand, he stood on the other side of her table with a smile in his eyes. God, she thought, this man was smooth. "And how, dear sir, do you know I am beautiful?" She had to smile in spite of the interruption to her conversation with TOM. It wasn't like this man had a clue. He looked familiar.

**You saw him sitting two rows behind Nathan when you left your sleeping cabin.**

She had forgotten TOM saw and remembered everything, but it was damn useful right now. So long as he didn't become an "I told you so" pain in the ass, she would deal with it.

"Madam, anyone who would block their beauty to save the rest of us from the sadness of no longer being permitted to view their face is not only beautiful on the outside, but is truly beautiful inside."

No wonder American women loved Europeans. While it was so much bullshit, they made it smell as wonderful as flowers in springtime. She reached out to accept the wine, and the gentleman sat down. The waiter was right there to take away her extra glass. She took a sip of the wine.

**Bethany Anne, this wine has an additional chemical compound that was not present in the one you just drank.**

Bethany Anne frowned, not letting the concern reach her eyes.

*What do you mean?*

**I mean this wine has other chemicals the wine you originally drank did not. Let me see what it is doing to you, and I'll let you know.**

*You do that.*

"May I introduce myself?"

"First names only, please."

He smiled. "Certainly. My name is Rafael, and yours?" He seemed to become even more sure of himself as he sat down. Was that due to her acceptance or something he put in the wine?

"Bethany Anne."

*TOM, hurry the fuck up.*

"How has your trip been so far? Are you going to Romania or returning to Romania? You are an American, correct?"

"Going back, Rafael, and yes, I'm an American."

**Got it, Bethany Anne. It is a set of chemicals that are working on your cognitive ability, making you less able to function. You would have started seeing effects about twenty to thirty minutes after you'd drunk the wine.**

*Can you get rid of it?*

Absolutely.

*Okay, TOM, I am upgrading you to less-than-pain-in-the-ass status.*

**Does this mean I move off the couch?**

*Hell, no.*

**Well, I tried.**

Bethany thought through her options. When she slipped into "vamp speed," everything slowed down around her and she was able to complete a significant amount of activity, physical or mental. Considering this asswipe had just tried to roofie her, one of her options was to throw him off the train while it was still rolling. But with her luck, they would do some sort of passenger count, find out they had a missing person, and stop the train. Of course, he could be working for someone and trying to kidnap her.

She still liked option one. Violence was never too far from the top of her preferred options.

Her voice became silk over steel.

"Tell me, Rafael, what is your real name?"

The man first started to look scared, then his whole face took on an almost blank expression.

"Paul. Paul Rutherford."

"So, you're not Spanish at all, are you?"

"Part. My mother was Spanish and my father was English, but we lived in France."

"And what were you expecting to do with me, Mr. Rutherford?"

"Once you were under the effects of the drug, I was going to have you come to my sleeping cabin for the night. There, I was going to go through your purse and steal your money and credit cards. I would have you share with me your PIN codes, as well."

"How many times have you done this, Mr. Rutherford?"

"Three times."

"Why have you not been reported and apprehended?"

"The ladies don't remember because of the drug, and I stop using the cards within seventy-two hours. They are often too embarrassed to pursue it with the law."

Bethany Anne switched their glasses of wine. "Drink up, Mr. Rutherford. I think you are about to have a poor night."

Paul drank the glass of wine, almost finishing it in one long gulp.

After getting his sleeping cabin number, she commanded him to go and sleep in his cabin and stay there until the train reached his stop. At that time, he was to go to the nearest police officer and admit his crimes. He stood to leave, and when he turned around, he bumped into Nathan coming down the car. Paul ignored Nathan and stepped around him, making a beeline toward his sleeper.

"What was that all about?" Nathan sat down.

"He just tried to roofie me. He dropped Rohypnol into the wine he bought me. Apparently, he has a small dick and a smaller amount of talent. He finds rich women susceptible to a few good lines and slips them a drug-laced drink."

Nathan kept a completely blank face.

"Nathan, shut up. I was trying to be nice to someone. He interrupted my thoughts, and I was trying not to be a raging bitch to the man, and look what that got me."

"I'm surprised you didn't throw him off the train. Without his arms."

"I considered it. I'm *still* considering it, actually. I know where he sleeps."

"I take it the drugs don't affect you?"

"Not the small amount I drank before I... Well, before I determined that he slipped the drug into the wine." She wasn't going to let him know TOM was the one who'd figured it out.

**Thanks a lot. I get no appreciation.**

*Shut up, or it's back to the doghouse.*

**Fine, fine.**

"That's a piece of good news. Maybe the only good news for a minute or two. So, I have bad news and even worse news. Which do you want first?" Nathan got the waiter's attention and found out they had both steak and lamb available. He ordered both with a double side of vegetables.

Bethany Anne raised her eyebrow at his double order of vegetables.

"Don't say a word. Just...don't."

She pinched her fingers together and made as if to zip her mouth shut. It was the least she could do considering Nathan had suggested ripping Mr. Rutherford's arms off. It was a stellar idea, and she was giving it some serious thought.

## CHAPTER 5

**Zurich, Switzerland to Brasov, Romania**

They sat at their table in companionable silence while Bethany Anne had a fresh glass of wine delivered. A minute later, the waiter was back with his food. Nathan, she noticed, had very good table manners.

He gave her a discreet update while he ate. "Our DC contact is having a lot of problems. He's lost a number of men without Bill's support in the dangerous operations. He's getting heat from higher-ups in the law enforcement/military hierarchy since he can't provide any resources except information. The rest of the family won't talk to him without Carl as a go-between, so no one here in Europe is getting any help either. The problems are starting to jam up, and after so many deaths, it won't be long before someone is going to realize there's been a substantial increase in deaths with unexplainable causes."

Finishing his meat, he started on his vegetables. "Now we move to Gerry, who's having a problem with the young and stupid and full of testosterone within the Were community. They've never liked the rules Michael put in place. The rumor mill is full of speculation that Michael is dead and no one from the vampire community has squelched that rumor in America, so the Council is having more and more problems keeping a lid on the troublemakers. At least here, the Council has had an incident with vampire involvement. Well, involved proactively. Everyone knows if you go and tweak a vampire, you should have your life insurance paid up. But in the States, the problem has been that they aren't doing anything without direction from Michael, or Carl in this case."

"Stephen isn't awake, supposedly, and Barnabas hasn't been seen in a dozen years or more. Peter is awake in Asia, but he takes care of that area without Michael's involvement. The last one, David, has been over in Russia for the last five years and I have no information on him. I know he has one more, but I can't remember his name."

Bethany Anne set her drink down. "I'll have a discussion with Stephen. He isn't on my good list since he hasn't been paying attention. Petre was a fine example. I'll get him motivated."

"How do you plan to do that? It isn't like you can just throw him into the sun like Petre. He's the only other vampire the sun doesn't affect."

"Nathan, everyone has a pressure point. If they don't, and I can't trust them, then I can always elevate someone else within the organization if a sudden opening at the top of the family occurs."

"You know, you kinda scare me when you do that."

"What?"

"Act like Michael. With him, killing is always the first, last, and potentially the only solution."

"Nathan, I don't want killing to be my first choice, but at the moment, it's the only punishment most of the family seems to understand."

The waiter approached, and they kept quiet while he took Nathan's plates and returned with coffee for them both.

Bethany Anne continued, "You should notice that Michael

had a weak spot. Except for the Forsaken, he hasn't directly punished his children when they've exhibited less than exemplary conduct."

"How would you attempt to do that? No offense, but going after Stephen, Barnabas, or any of the rest is going to be too much for you."

"Nathan, have you ever had any kids?"

"Yes, but I lost him in Vietnam."

Bethany Anne was reminded just how old Nathan really was. He looked like he was in his late twenties or a very young thirty. "Sorry to hear that. Did you have any problem punishing him?"

Nathan sat back, thinking back over the years when his son grew up. "Yeah. They say little girls can tie their fathers around their fingers. It was good that Adam wasn't a girl, but he had me tied up pretty good anyway. His mother had to punish him because I'd just slap his hand."

"Then you understand Michael's situation. He recognized a character trait in himself that wasn't working for everyone, so he made a change."

"That change is you? How is bringing in a sister going to change the brothers?"

"That's just it, Nathan. I'll let you in on a secret, one you will keep on pain of death. He didn't create a sister, but rather a mother. As his mother, I'm about to school Stephen on how upset 'Mom' really is."

Nathan could see her eyes glowing red behind her veil. *Oh, fuckity-fuck*, he thought. He had been concerned when he believed Bethany Anne to be a powerful vampire for her age, someone Michael might have a "talk" with when, and if, he ever came back. Now he wasn't sure Michael could or even would correct her if he came back.

Nathan desperately needed Gerry and the Council to get the troublemakers in line and circle the damn wagons. He was pretty sure that if Bethany Anne had to come fix things, it would be a bloodbath they would still talk about in another hundred and fifty years.

### Brasov, Romania

Ecaterina was in the hotel room waiting for Bethany Anne and Nathan to get back. Ivan had gone to pick them up at the train station. She was emotionally tired from arguing with her mother.

Why was it that mothers pushed their expectations of themselves onto their children? Ecaterina had never wanted a small house, a husband, and two children. She had never played house while growing up. She had always been outside, or away on the mountain with her father. That her mother had continued to try to force Ecaterina into the mold of a family woman was a testament to her ability to ignore reality.

When the time came to speak with her parents, Ecaterina's mother tried a massive guilt trip, complete with crying. When that had failed to work, her mother told her father he needed to talk some sense into his daughter. She went on to explain how bad his life would be if he didn't help her change Ecaterina's mind. It almost broke Ecaterina's heart to see her dad torn between two women he loved. Her dad had chosen to live with one, though, so as much as she loved him, she couldn't take that burden off his shoulders.

In the end, her mother simply went to her room and shut the door. Her father had helped Ecaterina put her luggage into Ivan's Mercedes. He looked at her with a small smile on his face.

"This is what you are, Katia. Your mother will fulfill her life through one of your siblings. Maybe Ivan, if he is able to stop helping every pretty woman and choose one, yes?" He smiled at Ivan, who had a long-suffering look on his face.

"She wants to have grandchildren, and she expected them from you. I told her before this wouldn't happen, and she told me I would see she was right. Well, now you are leaving, and worse, she knows I was right. I'm sure she will calm down eventually. Don't worry about me. I'll just go to the mountain for a few nights if I need some peace and quiet. But don't forget about us, okay? Send us an update to let us know what is going on."

She had promised her father she would email them from time to time. She didn't know where she was headed, but she expected to end up in America.

Her father started asking Ivan questions about Bethany Anne and Nathan—especially Nathan. His questions got so embarrassing that Ecaterina blushed furiously and started to get angry at her father. He merely winked at her and said goodbye, and they left.

She was embarrassed. Her father had baited her, and she'd responded. Now he knew she liked Nathan after she had spent all night working hard to keep the focus on Bethany Anne. *Gott Verdammt!*

## Constanta, Romania

Bethany Anne decided to have Nathan take Ecaterina to America. She didn't want any potential hostages around when she schooled Stephen's family.

She passed a message on to Frank that they would talk when she got back to the States. She used some of Nathan's connections. He was useful to have around to get some bonafide passports. With the contacts in Switzerland, she now had a legal Swiss passport. Frank had gotten word to her that he would have a US passport waiting for her in England that she could pick up on her way to DC.

It was amazing how much power a few billion dollars and over a trillion in assets provided someone. This was a little more than she was prepared to handle. She would need a damn team of

QUEEN BITCH

accountants to figure it all out. She had no idea how Michael had done it.

Once Ecaterina and Nathan were safely on their way, she went to track down Stephen and give him the talk. Without Nathan around to caution her, she grew a little angrier each time she remembered the way he had let Petre act. He hadn't taken responsibility for his loose cannon.

It took her three days to finally find his home, and what a home it was. Three stories tall, made of beautiful stone that looked like marble in the countryside outside of Constanta, Romania. The city was gorgeous, with streets that were paved with bricks from hundreds of years ago and bike racks set up for people to simply grab a bike and go. Bethany Anne had wanted to walk around and see more, but she felt the pressure of getting back to America as soon as possible to handle the situations Frank was dealing with.

While trying to find Stephen's house, she had thought she should, once again, follow the money. She found the oldest three banks in town and visited the first two to open accounts. After dropping a million US dollars, she was introduced to the banks' presidents. When she admitted she might have more she could deposit if she felt so inclined, they had bent over backward to answer her questions. She hit the jackpot at the second bank. The president had admitted his bank had a very wealthy patron by the name of Stephen who had no last name, and he would be happy to give her the address and a letter of introduction to pass to him. She thanked him for the help and left.

After lunch, it took a few minutes to capture the attention of a taxi driver. She had the driver leave her at a gas station about half a mile from the road that went past Stephen's house.

She admired the view as she walked up to the house and rang the doorbell. It was a real fucking bell, too. She pulled a rope that passed through a hole above the door and listened to the answering toll within. After pulling the rope three times and waiting twenty minutes, she considered banging on—or down—the front door. Finally, she heard slow steps approaching. The locks were turned, and a wizened old man stood in front of her.

If her nose hadn't confirmed it—to TOM as well—she wouldn't have believed she was staring at Michael's son Stephen.

He was old. Not like "Grandpa, stop looking at the girls, it's gross" old. He was "in the grave, just close the coffin lid" old. He had sunspots on his bald head, and his eyes looked like they had a light gray film on them.

*What the fuck?*

"Yes?" His voice was a little wheezy but not too bad.

"Stephen?" She couldn't help herself. She had expected someone…younger.

"Yes?"

Well, what the fuck was she supposed to do now? If she bitch-slapped Grandpa, she might break his fool neck, and although that wasn't really a consideration, she didn't feel like hitting this bag of bones.

"Do you have something to say, or shall I close this door, young woman?"

Yeah, that was right. He couldn't smell anything vampy about her. Hell, he might not be able to smell anything at all.

"May I come in? I have some news you might want to hear. It's about Petre."

"Yes, of course. What has that little miscreant done now?" Stephen turned around and walked back into the house. He had let his live-in caretakers go five years before. He still had his groundskeepers come weekly, and a housecleaning service came once a month to take care of dusting the house and vacuuming—tasks that wouldn't wake him up in the basement.

Bethany Anne looked around. It was clean, but obviously, no one lived here. They sat in the front room. It had ten-foot-high ceilings and floor-to-ceiling drapes along one wall. A Roman bust sat on a pedestal in the corner. The furniture looked hundreds of years old. Shit, it might be his *original* furniture.

She got to the point. "That miscreant used the Brasov Were pack as his personal gang of hoodlums, and they tried to assassinate an American Pack Council representative and a couple of locals. A human and a werebear who lived on the mountain were caught in the attack and were also going to be killed."

"Well, what do you want me to do about it?" Stephen was still trying to wake up. This woman was beautiful, but he was far past the stage where beautiful women did much for him.

"Nothing. I killed him."

Stephen jolted at that, and his eyes widened. "You?" The film receded from his eyes as he woke up. "How? Why?"

"The how was by pulling him into the sun a little at a time when he wouldn't—or couldn't—answer my questions, and the why was because he was being a little shit. Oh yeah, and he shot me."

Stephen was awake now. "When was this?"

"A couple of weeks ago."

"You don't look like you've been shot."

"I heal really fast. You should know. Hell, Petre was healing fast too. That was why I kept hitting him with the cricket bat. Well, that and I was pissed about getting shot. Did I mention the little shit shot me in the back?"

Stephen's eyes creased a little. "You don't smell like you should have been able to do that. You smell…normal. Why should I believe you?"

"You want me to come over there and let you get a better smell?" She raised an eyebrow, daring him to accept her offer.

"I'll take you up on that, young lady."

Bethany Anne walked over to Stephen and offered her wrist. In her last step, she switched to vamp speed, and the world went into super-slow motion. She let her arm hang about a foot from Stephen's face.

She saw the moment Stephen decided he would get a bite of that juicy wrist and his incisors started growing. He tried to launch himself off the couch and grab her arm with both his hands to bring her wrist up to his mouth.

She didn't want him to get his teeth in her. She knew she could eventually pry him off, but it would be a pain, and she was sure her Etheric energy would get drained. And while turnabout was fair play, the thought of drinking his geriatric blood just grossed her out.

So she grabbed his forehead with her left hand and pushed it back. Pulling her right hand close to her chest, she was able to do a quick twist and break his hold. Then she popped him in his right ear, and he shot away to land fifteen feet into the foyer. She walked over to him. Stephen lay on the ground, moaning, with his hands covering his ears.

"Why did you hit an old man like that?"

"I'm going to break your old-man legs if you don't stop acting like a fucking moron. Grow a fucking backbone, Stephen. I expected more from Michael's child."

He looked up at her, suddenly realizing he was playing with someone who was not only aware of the UnknownWorld but also knew who Michael was and how he was related to him. Which meant she had to have had an idea of how powerful he might have been if he had rejuvenated in the last few hundred years.

She had come alone and had just boxed his ears.

"What do you want?"

"I want you to get off your bony ass and have a real conversation with me. You're a pathetic excuse for a family head. What the hell has gotten into you?"

"You want to know?" Stephen got up gingerly and walked with decorum to the living room. At least in there, the floors were carpeted if he got a beat down again. She had been able to easily break his hold, so he didn't have a chance of overpowering her right now. Maybe after rejuvenation… Maybe!

"Yes. I not only want to know, but dammit, I need to." Bethany Anne sat near Stephen to show him she wasn't overly concerned with his attacking her again, and giving him something she felt he desperately needed—attention.

They ended up talking through the night. By dawn, it was obvious Stephen was drowning in loneliness. He also needed Etheric energy in a bad way. He was so weak a teenager might be able to kill him.

She considered what she could do about that. When she had arrived at the house, she'd thought she would have to kick his ass and probably kill him. Now, she wanted—no, she *needed*—to save him. Save him both physically and emotionally, since he was hurting horribly. He cared, and it was his Achilles heel. He was hiding from his troubles by sleeping, and he didn't want to create another child so he could grow young again.

*TOM, is there any way to safely move some of my Etheric energy to Stephen without endangering me?*

**Yes. You could give him some of your blood.**

*I am not letting those geezer fangs bite me. Hell, no.*

**Cut your wrist and let some drain into a bowl or a mug. He can drink it from there.**

*What about the nanocytes that are in me? What will they do to him?*

**They usually follow the three stages, remember? His body doesn't need to be made ready like for stages two and three, so they should just make him younger. I doubt there are enough nanocytes in a mug of blood to do much for him, though. Depending on how much Etheric energy you can provide, that would probably do the most good.**

*So the nanocytes aren't going to super-program him?*

**Uhhhhh, one second.**

Bethany Anne's head started to hurt. TOM was accessing the

organic computer in her brain. One of these fucking weeks, she would hole up and fix her connections. She wouldn't allow TOM to access the computer because it hurt so much, but she couldn't get information without the computer. It sucked.

About ten seconds later, the pain started to recede.

**Okay, I can use some of the Etheric energy and reprogram the nanocytes so they don't make any additional changes.**

*Wait! We can ask them to do additional changes?*

**Well, possibly. What do you have in mind?**

*Can you program them to have a back door or something?*

**What is a back door?**

*In this case, something we can contact through the Etheric and have them change routines if we want?*

She waited through another bit of silence from TOM.

**Yes. We can at least get them to communicate their location if you want. I'm not sure how much more. I hadn't considered that.**

*That will have to be good enough. If I can figure out where he is, I should be able to figure out if he's doing what I want.*

Bethany Anne stood up and moved into the kitchen, and Stephen watched her with curiosity. Although he was physically tired, his brain was awake. It had been many, many decades since he had talked with anyone who he felt safe sharing secrets with. The strictures limited him to talking with his siblings, who were spread all over the world. He felt bad about what Petre had been up to, but it seemed this woman had taken care of that. He hadn't wished ill on Petre, but he had gone against the strictures when he shot this woman. Petre's poor judgment lay in not finding out more about her. He should not have shot anyone connected with Michael, and had Stephen been informed, he would have been required to kill Petre for his actions. She had saved him the anguish of killing one of his children.

She didn't seem to have many hang-ups. She knocked him on his ass without blinking. He wondered if her generation didn't appreciate what it took to live this long, or if she would have hit him before she had been transformed.

She looked around the kitchen until she found a filleting knife, grabbed a mug from above the sink, and took them into the living room. She glanced around. She didn't want to make a mess, but she would lose the value of the effort if she didn't do this right in front of him.

She set the knife and the mug between them on the coffee table. He sat up on the couch and looked at the mug and knife and back up at her.

"Stephen, I appreciate all you have shared with me. Know first that *I am not Michael*. If I make a pact with you, you can be sure I will do whatever is in my power to honor it. I need a powerful Nacht here in Europe. I need you to come back to the living again, Stephen. To wake up and stay awake. I need you to be my eyes and ears here in Europe. I need you to be strong again, Stephen. For me, for the Nacht, and frankly, for the world. Will you accept this gift of my blood—blood that will strengthen you and connect you to me? And will you work with me to make this world better for the Nacht, for the UnknownWorld, and for the humans as well?"

Stephen looked into her eyes, those beautiful eyes he imagined had glowed as he told her his story through the night. She had become his priestess, his sister, and his friend. Would he? Would he be willing to do this? For the humans? No. He didn't have enough love for any humans or Weres right now. Maybe in the future. But for Bethany Anne? For Bethany Anne, he would do this, and he would follow her until the grave finally claimed his body.

He placed his frail arm over his chest. "Yes, my lady. I will do this as you ask. But know I am from centuries past. I know you don't ascribe to the old ways, ways that were old hundreds of years before you were born. But if you would let me drink from your wrist, I will be your servant until the end of my days, whether that be today or a thousand years in the future."

Bethany Anne looked down at the mug and knife and realized it was a poor substitute for the ritual request of Stephen's allegiance. If she was going to be a queen, the Queen of the UnknownWorld, it would not be done with a porcelain mug and a filleting knife.

She stood up and walked over to Stephen, who looked up into her eyes as she stood next to him. "Drink, Stephen. Swear your allegiance to me, and I will provide you sustenance. But if you don't stop when I tell you, I will put my fist through your skull. Do you understand me?"

"Yes, my Queen. I understand."

She offered her wrist and Stephen took it lovingly. Slowly, ever so slowly, he pierced her vein with his fangs, making sure he was beyond careful with this woman who had saved him from the mortality of loneliness and given him new hope and a new reason to live.

When she tapped him gently on the head about five minutes later, his mind and his body were abuzz. The blood was changing him. Changing him *again*, it felt like. Every point of light in the room was bright.

"Lie down, Stephen, and sleep. I will protect you while you rest. You have my word."

Stephen closed his eyes and was instantly all but comatose. Bethany Anne pulled his legs up on the couch and searched the house until she found a blanket. She wasn't sure he needed it, but it might be a comfort, and she wanted to tuck him in. Then she went back to the chair across from him and sat down.

*Michael's family is sure dysfunctional,* she thought.

She had learned that TOM had the ability to pay attention to what was going on around her, even when she wasn't paying attention—like when he was able to pinpoint where she had seen Paul Rutherford on the train. She had confirmed with him later that he was constantly paying attention to all her senses, and learning more about the world as he went along. He was very smart, but ignorant about Earth customs, and was constantly pulling in information to try to understand. Considering it was becoming more dangerous for her should she be caught unawares, she needed TOM to keep track of what she didn't.

She missed Nathan's guard dog sensibilities and hoped he and Ecaterina were doing all right.

She got up and went to the front door to make sure all the locks were in place. Going back to the closet where she had gotten the blanket for Stephen, she took another for herself and sat back down in the chair. She asked TOM to take the first watch. She then had to explain that people would break up the night into watches so some could sleep while others would stay awake to protect them. He told her he would be glad to take the first, second, and third watches. It wasn't like he slept anyway.

She closed her eyes and rested. Emotionally drained, she was out in seconds.

CHAPTER 6

**Constanta, Romania**
**Bethany Anne, I sense that Stephen is waking up.**

Bethany Anne opened her eyes, assessing the room quickly. Nothing had changed. She was still in the chair, and Stephen still lay on the couch.

*How?*

**His heartbeat just increased by ten percent. It is an anomaly that hasn't happened the entire time he has been asleep.**

*So, his heartbeat changed and you're ready to say he's waking up?*

She stood up and peered down at Stephen. He was looking a lot better.

While he still looked old, his face seemed a little less like a skull with leather skin, flushed and fuller. His skin had lost all the sunspots, marks, and blemishes, and he looked about ten years younger.

His eyes suddenly opened, startling her.

"Hey, you're awake."

Stephen looked around and sat up. He looked at the blanket over his body and back up at Bethany Anne.

"I couldn't let you just lie there like a cord of wood. I didn't know if you got cold, so I found the linen closet and borrowed a couple of blankets."

"Thank you. It has been a really long time since I have been looked after. Maybe centuries."

Bethany Anne smiled. "Trust me, I'm happier to have looked after you while you slept than to have to knock some sense into you." She went back and sat down in her chair.

"I truly think you would have done just that."

She sighed. "Yes. I have become a little jaded since it seems the only thing vampires understand is violence—lots and lots of violence—so I expected to come here and have to drag you outside to get your attention. I knew you could walk in the sun, but I figured it would wake you up."

"May I ask what you would have done then?"

"Well, I assumed I'd have to yank off one of your arms and beat you with it until I got your attention. Frankly, after that, I was going to play it by ear. I was rather hoping you would be a reasonable guy, but from the stories I heard, I wasn't giving that a very high probability."

Stephen looked at his new Queen for a minute. She was such a dichotomy between gentle on the one hand and violent on the other. She would make a very good Queen, he decided. He truly was happier than he had been in centuries. His time of loneliness —since Michael had gone to the New World—was over. For her, he would even get on a plane to go visit. Although he had never flown, he now had a reason to.

"What will you do now, Stephen? I've got to go back to America for a while. I'll need to come back over here, I'm sure, if for no other reason than to talk to you. How do you keep up your grounds while you hibernate?"

"I have people." He left out that they were merely an agency he had set up a decade before and hadn't spoken to since.

"Okay, I see you're looking better. How are you going to—" Bethany Anne stopped. She didn't know what it took to get younger again.

"Rejuvenate?"

"Is that what you call it, to look young again?"

"Yes. In order for us to make our bodies young again, we have to consume a significant quantity of blood and exchange it with another. This process turns them into a vampire and turns their parent young again."

"Do you force this change on others?" Bethany Anne wasn't sure she could allow this. In fact, she *knew* she couldn't allow it. There had to be a different way.

"No, no one in Michael's family would force a change. He has enacted certain rules we adhere to. One of them is, the person must understand their options, and another is—"

Bethany Anne finished the sentence with him, "They can only have six months to live. Yeah, I got that one." She started biting the inside of her cheek, which was an old habit when she was thinking.

"You've been asleep pretty long, right? You don't have anyone whom you know wants to go through this process and is ready. Shit, this is going to be a tough nut to crack." Bethany Anne got up and started pacing. She thought better while she moved.

***TOM, what really turns the vampire body back to young again? Is it the blood, or is it the Etheric energy that much blood gives them?***

**It would be the energy. The age has to do with the cells decaying. With that much energy, the nanocytes would be able to accomplish stage one again.**

***So, if we connected Stephen to an Etheric energy battery, he would be able to do the same thing, right? Basically, doing a blood***

***transfusion...*** Bethany Anne realized she had an answer...possibly.

"Stephen, have the vampires ever consumed blood from a blood bank?"

He looked at her and thought about it. "*I* haven't. Since I don't talk to my siblings, I can't answer for them. If something like that works, I don't imagine they would share the information."

"Why not?"

"We might be siblings, as in children of Michael, but we compete with each other and frankly, we guard our secrets. It's one of the reasons we don't really talk to each other."

Bethany Anne started down that logic path. If one—or more —of the vampires really studied blood, they would probably be able to identify the components that connected to the Etheric. Maybe they didn't understand *how* it worked, but what it accomplished might have been enough. With as much genetic research as had taken place in the past four decades, she imagined a lot of information was available. Since Stephen, and Michael for that matter, had ignored humanity and stayed hibernating, they wouldn't know much about the advances in science.

"Okay, I think I have an answer. Let me research this a little more." She got out her smartphone and made sure she had a signal.

"What is that?"

"Hmm? Oh, this is a phone that is able to connect to the Internet. From there I can pull up information, something like books in a library anywhere in the world."

"Really? I've been asleep too long. I have no knowledge of this."

"I know, trust me. First, I need to get you younger, fast. Then I need to get you up to speed with reality and connect you with the EPC."

"EPC?"

Bethany Anne put the phone to her ear. "European Council of Weres." She put up a finger to hold his next question.

"Hi, this is Bethany Anne. I read on a website that Lithuania has four blood donation sites and you pay about twelve Euros for each donation, for about 63,000 donations a year. Is that right? Yes, yes, I'm willing to make a donation. No! I don't want to donate blood. I want to purchase blood for a financial donation. How much? Well, let's see. There are about five liters of blood in a body, right? Okay, how about five thousand Euros for twenty-five liters of blood?"

"Yes, I am looking to make a donation of five thousand Euros for twenty-five liters. It has to be flown to me tonight. I'll pay all the fees necessary if you will get it to—" She put her hand over the phone.

"Stephen, what's a good place to get a delivery around here? I don't want it coming directly to your house."

"We can use the hospital. I have a foundation that provides them money every year. They will do this for me."

"Really? That's incredible. Remind me to let you know you're my new favorite vampire." She removed her hand from the phone and told them what hospital she wanted it delivered to.

Twenty minutes later, she got a return call. They had made a deal with the hospital to take the twenty-five liters of blood out of their stores, and they would resupply the hospital within forty-eight hours. It cut down on the costs of transportation, and they could access the blood right away.

Bethany Anne smiled. It was nice to have something go right for once. Now, stretching her luck a little, she made a phone call to Brasov.

A man's voice answered the phone. "Hello?"

"Ivan, this is Bethany Anne."

"Hello! How is my favorite…uh…lady?" Ivan stammered a little when he realized he couldn't say some things out loud.

"I'm good. Hey, do you want to do your favorite lady a favor, and get paid for it?"

"Probably, but you know you took my negotiator out of the country, right? You wouldn't take advantage of me, knowing my weakness for dimples, would you?" Ivan's smile could be heard through the phone.

"Of course not. Tell you what, I'm going to need you to come to the coast to teach my friend how to use technology. Cell phones, the Internet, computers—all of it. If you could be here by tomorrow morning, that would be fantastic. Can you do that for me? I swear I have dimples showing right now."

Ivan laughed. "Even for you, tomorrow morning is a little too soon. Could it be tomorrow afternoon? I need to meet with a couple of people before I leave. How long will you need me?"

Bethany Anne looked at Stephen and considered what he had told her last night. "Uh, plan on a couple of months. He is not so up-to-date."

"Is he educated? This isn't for a female? I could get there even sooner for a female. Well, maybe not. If you need me for that long, I'm going to need to talk to another friend and let my dad know I'm going to be gone."

"What about your mom?"

"She still isn't talking to us. I think now she is embarrassed and her pride isn't allowing her to say, 'I'm sorry.'"

"Well, I hope that solves itself before you get back to Brasov. You know you could just marry some girl to fix it, right?"

"Oh, God, no! I will call Dad on my way out of town. Thank you for reminding me what might happen if my mom hears about this. You said I'll get paid?"

"Yes. I know how badly you screwed Nathan over. How could you charge him that much?"

"Hey, I was looking out for Ecaterina. Rich American…what was I supposed to do?" Ivan was certainly smiling again.

"Yeah, okay. I'll tell you what. I'll pay the same amount for each week you're here helping my friend."

"And partial weeks?"

"Yes, and partial weeks!" Bethany Anne had to laugh. Ivan was in negotiation mode, and not even dimples would get her off the hook.

"Okay. Anything special I should know about your friend?"

"Well, his name is Stephen—"

"Bethany Anne, you did not just negotiate for me to teach technology to a…a…uh…"

"Yes, Ivan. I did. Now, be a man and own that you just got snookered by the dimples, and I'll see you tomorrow."

"Okay, but I'm holding you accountable if I'm not safe."

Bethany Anne was able to smile. "Ivan, you'll be one of the safest men in Romania while you're here. I guarantee it!"

They hung up.

"Stephen, let's go to the hospital. I feel like a miracle is about to happen."

"How do you want to get there?"

"Let me guess, you don't have a car?"

"I do. I did learn how to drive, but probably the gas is bad after this many years."

She pulled her phone out again. "Well, let's use this miracle device to get a taxi."

Stephen couldn't help it. With Bethany Anne around, he found he was rather looking forward to living again. His hope had been rekindled.

"By the way, Stephen?"

"Yes?"

"If anything happens to Ivan, I will come back over here and beat the shit out of you with your own arms."

"My lady, if anything happens to Ivan while I am around, I'll already be dead."

"That's what I wanted to hear."

"I understand. I'll not fail you."

For once, Bethany Anne felt like there was a little light at the end of the tunnel, at least here in Europe. They continued to talk about what changes needed to happen and had switched to normal topics when the taxi arrived.

### Constanta, Romania

The hospital was almost a non-event. When they showed up, it was still early evening, so the hospital administrator was on the premises. When Stephen explained that as the foundation's executor, he wanted to see how the hospital was using their funding, he immediately received preferential treatment.

Bethany Anne was amazed to see how much better he was getting. He moved like a spry seventy-year-old as they walked around the hospital. She had her hat on again; she loved the air of mystery it provided her.

Plus, she looked damn good in it.

Stephen was overjoyed with her company, and wouldn't allow Bethany Anne to do anything but be on his arm the whole way through their tour. He knew she approved of his funding the hospital and was very proud that he could make her happy. In the end, Bethany Anne switched her voice and gave the administrator instructions to have someone place twenty-five liters of the freshest blood in a secure room and leave it there. She then told him to work at least three more hours and waited in the room with Stephen until the blood was delivered. She 'told' the hospital worker the blood had been picked up, and he couldn't remember by whom.

Once the worker was gone, she turned to Stephen.

"Okay, I have some information to give you. I am trusting you with this information and expect you to keep it a secret unless I tell you otherwise, or if in your best judgment, the risk is worth the reward. Do you understand?"

"Yes, of course." He looked at the quantity of blood. It was a lot of blood. Much more than he could possibly drink.

"As you know, when you change a human, the act of making them a vampire rejuvenates you. What you don't realize is, there are infinitesimally small genetic machines inside your body that need the energy to work. When you suck the blood out of another human and then force it back into their body, what you are doing is putting the machines into their body, and those machines then turn them into a vampire. For you, however, it provides your nanocytes with needed energy so they can fix your body. This is what turns you young.

"When you exchange the blood with a human, you drain four or five liters of blood at a time. I purchased twenty-five liters because I don't know how potent the blood is and how much energy you will need."

TOM chose that moment to interrupt.

**Bethany Anne, you might make this easier by mixing your blood with the bagged blood. If we wait a little while, the nanocytes will start propagating in the blood mix and possibly make it more effective.**

She thought this through. She didn't want Stephen to have too many of her nanocytes, but she didn't want to be here all night, either. She was pretty sure the Etheric energy was gathered by the whole body, not merely the blood where it was focused.

"Okay, Stephen, I want you to start taking the blood. I am going to mix one of these bags with mine, and depending on how long it takes, you'll consume it later."

It took two hours for Stephen to consume three of the bags of blood. The fourth liter was the one Bethany Anne had mixed her blood with two hours before.

Even before he took the last bag, he looked like he had dropped another twenty years.

By the end of the fourth bag, which took another two hours since it was very difficult for him to consume any more, it was obvious he wouldn't need any extra blood.

"Huh, I guess I went overboard on this, didn't I?" She looked at the additional twenty-one bags in the coolers.

Stephen's vitality was up. It looked like he had just consumed a Thanksgiving turkey by himself.

"No, my lady. It won't go to waste. I will donate it back to the hospital, and ask them to set aside a revolving stock of fresh blood to be available twenty-four hours a day. If I had known rejuvenation was possible without needing to make a vampire, I might have considered doing this before—although I can't be sure. Until you came along, I was ready to just rest for the final time. I appreciate all you have done for me."

Bethany Anne smiled at him. "Don't worry, Stephen. You will work diligently to get Europe back on track. We are going to make this work, and work well. I'm happy to have been here to help you, and I'm happy I didn't have to rip your arm off." She patted him on the shoulder. "Ivan will be here tomorrow. He has a phone and knows my number. You know that small room next to the linen closet in your home?"

"Yes, I believe so. To the right or left?"

"Left. It has a small bed in it right now."

"Yes."

"Good. I want you to remove the bed and lock the door. Only allow someone to clean it once a quarter. If you need me, I'll come to you."

"How will you do that?"

Bethany Anne grabbed one of the packages of blood. "Why, like this." And then she disappeared.

Stephen stared at where she had been for a minute before realizing she could move her body instantly to different locations. She must need to be sure no one was in the same space in order to be safe. He would make sure the room was safe for her.

In fact, he decided, he would make sure all of Europe was safe for his Queen. He grabbed the cooler of blood under his arm and left the room. Even feeling overly full, there was no time like the present to get started.

CHAPTER 7

**Washington, DC, USA**

It was 3:30 in the afternoon when Frank's phone rang. Caller ID showed an unknown number.

"Hello, Frank Kurns."

"Hello, Frank, this is Bethany Anne."

He straightened in his chair. "Hello, Ms. Reynolds. I appreciate the phone call."

"Not Ms. Reynolds anymore, Frank. The Nacht don't have last names. We surrender them when we change."

It was a quick and efficient way to inform Frank that he wasn't speaking to the lady who left America. This was a new woman. A different woman altogether.

"Yes, I see." He really didn't, but he needed to get his game hat back on. For almost a year, he hadn't spoken to Carl or any of the vampires, and he remembered how particular they could be. "Bethany Anne it is, then. I appreciate your call. Are you here in the States?"

"No, I'm presently at a train station in Romania. I was considering taking a commercial flight back and realized we might be able to work together. I need a fast way back to America, but I'd like a flight where I'm not concerned about mayhem happening to random people. I know you want me back there to see how I might be able to help with both your operations and the Were problem. Do you happen to have a solution?"

"Um, mayhem?" What was she into already? What had she started that had the potential to cause mayhem on a commercial flight?

"Yes. It seems Mr. Lowell and I were tagged on a train from Switzerland to Romania, and I've had someone try Rohypnol on me already. While I know I can take care of myself, I tend to be a little extreme in the way I dish out retribution."

Frank considered his response. So, his guy had been made on the train, so he should come clean about that, and he needed to see what he could set up for a fast trip across the Atlantic.

"Well, I can update you on the train incident. I had an agent trying to find Nathan and you to get information on what was going on. Nathan talked to me during the trip, and I sent my guy a message to drop off before contact."

"Was his name Paul Rutherford?"

"No, it wasn't. Why?" Frank penciled the name Paul Rutherford with a question mark beside it on a scratch pad. He would look the man up later.

"Just confirming something."

"Okay, as for the transportation, I feel confident that I can get you here. I have an operation going down tomorrow night. If I can get you here in time, are you willing to take it on?"

"Most likely. What are the parameters?"

"We have a situation in the Florida Everglades. We think we have two Nosferatu down there. The alligators are getting the blame for people disappearing, and I can't have a major military effort. It's too obvious. My smaller team is good, but these guys have been on the sharp end of this stick four times in three months, and frankly, they are wiped. They've lost two men recently."

"We have Nosferatu in the US? Those ass-maggots. Yeah, I'll be happy to go down there and help them. Just make sure you have the right gear for me. I didn't buy any sets of 'Florida Everglades Fatigues,' and I'm not ruining my Louboutins in that swamp."

Frank wanted to pull his phone away from his ear and look at it. Ass-maggots? Bethany Anne was a whole lot different than the people he was accustomed to working with. He'd had a short voice message from Nathan this morning to treat her like the real deal and not piss her off.

Everyone had tried not to piss her off even when she was human. In light of her super-lethal abilities—then and now—anyone trying to piss her off was having a certifiable moment of stupidity. Frank hadn't lasted this many years by making mistakes like that.

But Nathan's advice had gotten him wondering how powerful she had actually become. Apparently, it hadn't taken her as long to grow into her powers as he'd thought it might.

"I'll call you back in fifteen minutes with the transportation details. Send me your clothing sizes, and I'll have someone get a set of fatigues ready for you."

"Okay, that works for me. I'll be at the main pickup location for the train station. Just a warning. Don't send an ass-munch to pick me up or you might not get him back. Bye." Bethany Anne hung up her cell phone and dropped the blood bag into a trashcan as she walked to the main pickup area.

Frank looked at his phone before hanging up and pulling up his computer. Yeah, she hadn't changed much from what his research had told him. Well...except now when she said "you might not get him back," he was pretty sure she didn't mean it figuratively.

He had to get busy if he wanted to make sure the team had the best chance for all of them to live through tomorrow night.

He sure hoped they remembered to mind their Ps and Qs

when she got there. She was a good-looking woman, and those SpecOps guys thought they walked on water. That might not fly with a woman who might just *be* able to walk on water.

### Atlantic Ocean

Bethany Anne had been picked up in a black sedan by a female captain. The captain asked no questions, was very polite to her and took her to an airfield about an hour and a half away. In the car were a flight suit and boots in Bethany Anne's size. She changed in the car, although she hated leaving her outfit behind. On impulse, she asked the captain if the car perhaps had a box anywhere so she could bring her change of clothes on the plane.

Looking a little confused, the woman explained that in a two-seat fighter jet there wasn't enough room to change your mind, much less carry an extra load of clothes. She would see that the box of clothes got shipped red-label FedEx the next morning.

Bethany Anne was a little surprised Frank would provide a fighter jet for her transportation. She later learned that pilots had to have enough flying hours. Her pilot was a little short for fighters, since he had mostly flown larger transportation planes, and when the chance came up to get some F-15 hours he'd jumped on it. Had he known he would fly a gorgeous model to the United States, he would have slit his wrists for the chance. She could hear the smile in his voice when he said this, but thankfully, it wasn't like some of the scuzzier comments she'd received when working in DC.

She took the compliment as it was intended and thanked him. They would refuel in the air and fly straight to Florida. Once in the air, she zoned out and allowed TOM to pay attention for a while. She noticed she lost her ability to 'feel' what direction Stephen was about midway across the Atlantic, but she could still tell he was alive. She wondered whether this ability would stay with her or if she would lose it as her blood worked its way through his system.

A couple of hours later, the pilot came over the headset and directed Bethany Anne's attention to the islands of the Azores as they passed over. The flight was peaceful, or at least as peaceful as it could be flying as fast as they were. She finally decided to simply go to sleep.

A few hours later, she woke up with the coast in the distance. She had missed the mid-air refueling, having completely zoned out. The pilot was amazed she had been able to sleep through the whole thing. All he knew about his passenger was that he needed to get her to Florida fast.

She was moved so quickly from his plane to the car that he didn't get a chance to ask for her phone number.

### New York City, NY, USA

Ecaterina looked at all the strange and exciting city lights. Nathan had brought her over on first-class tickets and made sure a limousine waited for them with her name on the placard when they came out of the security gate at John F. Kennedy.

Security had been a two-hour nightmare for them since Ecaterina had never before been out of her country.

Nathan finally managed to get them through security, and she was excited to be in the limousine. He had the driver go through Times Square. It added forty-five minutes to their trip, but he didn't care. Her face, radiant with delight, was all the payment he needed.

Ecaterina finally scooted close to him when they left Times Square. She gave him a shy smile and took his hand gently and rested her head on his shoulder, closing her eyes.

*My God*, he thought, *I love this woman.*

It had been over thirty years since Nathan had had any type of serious relationship. His first wife had suffered when their child had been killed in Vietnam, and she had never been the same. Although she had eventually gotten through her grief and a serious depression, she was never again the vivacious woman he had married.

She hadn't known about him being a Wechselbalg. It wasn't a serious problem, but it did mean Nathan was always aware that their relationship wasn't completely transparent. Now, due to Bethany Anne more than anyone, he had a chance to really enjoy a relationship, and this time there would be no secrets.

He felt like the most special pillow in the world at that moment as he listened to her breathing while she slept against him.

He quietly told the driver to take the very long way to his house. He had the money to make this last a little while longer, and he was going to do it.

---

Waking Ecaterina up in the limousine wasn't the struggle Nathan thought it would be. She was instantly alert and looked around quickly. He realized she was acting no different than she would out in the forest.

God, he *really* loved this woman.

The driver grabbed all the bags—only two of them were Ecaterina's—and dropped them on the doorstep of his brownstone. Two bags to move to another country. God, he really, *really* loved this woman.

What Nathan didn't know was that Bethany Anne had another three boxes being shipped over. Some of the things Ecaterina wanted to take along were not easy to transport on a commercial flight. They really frowned on firearms and ammunition. They weren't wild about traps, either.

Bethany Anne wasn't concerned, and since Ecaterina had an emotional attachment to the equipment, she got on her phone and rented a place outside Newark and had the boxes shipped there. Personally, she had an emotional attachment to the bear trap and had gone back to get it. She tracked it down to one of the Pack members, who was quick to give it up. They could never do something too fast for Bethany Anne. She supposed they might have finally made the link between the unknown vampire and her.

Nathan had paid and tipped the driver before walking Ecaterina up to the house. He had thought he might have to carry her in. Nope. In fact, she was ready to explore the neighborhood in the dark. He hoped the cleaning ladies had been there while he was gone. They did a good job, mostly. His only complaint was that they stuffed *everything* in his kitchen into the pantry. Every single time. It made his kitchen look pristine, but he would find moldy bread there a week later because he forgot he had it after they cleaned for him and would buy another loaf. Eventually, he smelled the bread and would find all the food and bring it back out. There was no telling what he would find this time.

He carried the bags inside as Ecaterina walked around the house, admiring the curios and knickknacks. He showed her to the guest bedroom on the first floor behind the kitchen. It had its own bathroom and shower, and a small closet. The bed in that room was the best in the house, so it was the room he gave to most of his visitors.

She smiled at him and gave him a peck on the cheek for bringing in her luggage. She hadn't expected him to, but being curious to see the house, she hadn't thought about it until it was too late.

"Thank you, Nathan. I'm sure I will only be here a few days until Bethany Anne arrives and we will be going...somewhere. She used to live in Washington DC. Is that far?"

He smiled at her. "No, maybe four or five hours by train. Shorter for a plane and car, of course. My home is your home.

Whatever you want, grab it. Don't make me tell you again, please?"

Her radiant smile remained with him as he climbed the stairs all the way to the third floor, where his room was located. He showered and got ready for bed. On the nightstands by the bed were two pictures. One of his son and him, and one with his wife, son, and him.

He grabbed the one with the three of them and looked down at it for a couple of minutes, then walked to his closet and pulled down a box of pictures. It was time to move on. Life had a way of healing all hurts in time. He put the picture frame in the box and replaced the lid.

He shut off the lights and went to sleep.

Down on the first floor, Ecaterina wished he had asked her to come upstairs. The distance between them seemed like a thousand miles. But still, she was happy. Impatient, yes, but very, very happy.

Hopefully, Bethany Anne wouldn't be finished too quickly, she thought as she turned off her lights to go to sleep.

## CHAPTER 8

**Everglades, FL, USA**
Bethany Anne was treated with kid gloves from the landing at the Air Force base to the forward operations center an hour and a half away. The jet taxied right into a hangar, where they picked her up in a blacked-out SUV. She felt like they were filming a Hollywood movie. She had to laugh at the whole scenario. Black SUV, black leather, bulletproof glass, and super-dark tint on the windows. Who did they think they were transporting?

As the only passenger in the back of the limited-edition Explorer—*Go, Ford*, she thought—she only had the driver and his shotgun to talk to. These guys were professionals. She asked why the tint was so dark on the windows, and they looked confused before Eric, the driver, admitted it was for her. The passenger, John, added that he was under the impression the "agents from her group" had an aversion to sunlight like their previous contact, Bill.

Eric wore a dark suit with a white shirt and dark red tie. John followed the prescribed dress code but substituted a classy medium-blue tie. At least they weren't MIB, she thought. Well fuck, maybe she represented MIB since she was the one with the alien.

"Did you guys work with Bill very often?" She hadn't been able to get Carl to open up about Bill on their flight to Romania, so she was curious about the agents' insights into a true vampire. While Bethany Anne knew everyone considered her a vampire, she wasn't one in the classic sense. Not what most considered a vampire to be, anyway.

John took over the conversation and let Eric focus on driving. "Yes, ma'am. I worked with him on eight operations or so. He was scary as hell—no offense, ma'am."

Bethany Anne delivered the following comment with the most sophisticated English accent she could pull off. "John, you're going to have to grow a fucking pair if you're going to cuss around me. There isn't a cuss word you butt-munchers have ever said that could possibly offend me, and I will give ten points to whoever can make me laugh."

Eric had to pull the SUV over to the side of the road. He laughed so hard tears flowed down his face, limiting his ability to see. John rolled in his seat. It didn't take long before the ops center radioed in, asking if everything was okay. Their GPS showed that they had stopped. The voice sounded a little worried.

Bethany Anne took the mic from Eric, who couldn't stop laughing long enough to answer the inquiry. With both her escorts incapacitated, she clicked the mic and spoke into it. "Ops center, this is Bethany Anne. I needed to stretch my legs after flying for so long. We will be back on the road in five." She clicked off the mic and stepped out of the vehicle to walk around, giving John and Eric a moment to compose themselves.

They had needed just this kind of catharsis after their last half a year. Frankly, the team needed all the help they could get, but they were on eggshells around Bethany Anne. They didn't know what kind of personality their contact would have. They knew she was a vampire, and they knew the type of creatures they were fighting.

Both John and Eric had been in the hangar when the fighter had taxied right through the door. As the canopy disengaged and pulled back, the passenger in the back stood up, turned around, and stepped down the stairs. Both had enough presence of mind not to say anything in case she was paying attention, but they had not realized they would pick up a female who made their eyes bug out.

She took off her helmet and handed it to the ground support guy, and John and Eric noticed he never closed his mouth. John watched as two others helped take off all the support pieces on her flight suit. She had waved to the pilot with a smile, then walked over to the SUV and got in.

Inside the car, John and Eric could hear the ops center ask no one in particular, "Did she just say she was going to walk around outside a bit?"

A few minutes later, Bethany Anne heard John roll down his window and speak in a normal voice. "Ma'am, we have our fucking shit together whenever you're ready." She smiled, turned back to the vehicle, and walked the fifty yards at a normal speed. No need to freak them out when she had just gotten them settled down.

She sat in the back seat. "Home, James." Both men smiled, and Eric pulled the SUV out onto the two-lane freeway and gunned the engine to try to make up the lost time.

*God*, John thought, *it feels good to have hope again*. The two agents spent the next hour telling her stories about their time with Bill, throwing in various cuss words to see if they could surprise her. They didn't, but she almost made Eric pull back off the road one more time. John was simply happy he wasn't driving.

. . .

## New York City, NY, USA

Gerry was going to strangle somebody before this day was through. He was presently in his office in Queens. Nathan had made it back the previous night and was supposed to arrive at midday. He'd taken a huge number of calls from the local pack for the last week while Nathan was out of town. Nirene had tried to help him, but the amount of butt-kissing required pissed him off.

He had assumed there wasn't a large amount of politics in his pack when he talked weekly with Nirene and Nathan. They'd never mentioned it. What he realized now was that the pack members had found out Nathan hated ass-kissing, intimidation, or any other form of manipulation. One idiot had tried blackmail, only to have all his darkest secrets exposed on his social media accounts.

Then he'd received an email from an anonymous source that told him his financial accounts would be hit next. Did he want to continue his blackmail effort? After the story got around, no one had considered trying blackmail on Nathan again.

Gerry's phone rang. It was another pack member who "just needed to see him."

Gerry's face broke into maybe the first genuine smile he'd had all week. "Max, I understand, but I am really busy today. Tomorrow? No, I'm not available tomorrow, but Nathan is back in town, and I am sure he'll talk to you. Should I tell Nathan you'll call? Don't bother? You'll get in touch with him? Fine, I'll let you do that."

Gerry hung up the phone and smiled in satisfaction. Maybe today wouldn't go so badly after all.

Now, if he could just throw Nathan at the Council's problems, life could get back to being good again. Unfortunately, as the Alpha of the Council, it was his burden to bear. Nathan had left him a short phone message that morning saying he hadn't found Michael, but if the Council didn't get their act together, they were going to wish he had. Gerry couldn't understand that message at all. Who would possibly make them wish for Michael to be back?

It couldn't be the new vamp, could it? He had heard rumors from Europe that she had been involved in the event in Brasov and had taken out another vampire, but he would wait until he got verification from Nathan before believing that.

Anyway, he would know more in a few hours.

### Everglades, FL, USA

Agent Dan Bosse heard the front tactical lookout—a euphemism for sniper—through his earpiece. "Sir, I have the vehicle in sight."

"Understood. How does everything look?" Dan hoped the sniper would report he had two living agents in the front seats. This contact was unknown, and although he had been told she wasn't a meat-eating monster, he was paid to worry and bring his men back alive. Unfortunately, that meant working with these contacts to help his crew take down other monsters which made even *his* men lose sleep at night. It was a shame he couldn't simply napalm the whole area and save his guys the risk of dying tonight.

Dan had worked with Bill for fifteen years, and during all the operations Bill had been part of he had only lost two men. Now, he had lost two men in the last month, not counting the others in the last twelve months.

After working with Bill for so long, his team had attributed more of the success to their part of the operations than they should have. He hated to admit it, but his guys were getting slaughtered. If he needed to work with a monster to take down other monsters, he would do it.

"Sir, I have them on scope, and you aren't going to believe this."

"Spit it out, Killian."

"Sir, the agents are laughing. I can see the pickup, and holy shit, sir, she is *hot*."

"Killian, keep it professional. If you mouth off around one of these agents, you could lose your head."

"Yeah, but what a way to go."

Dan shook his head. At least he had two agents alive and apparently in good spirits. It was the first piece of good news he had received that day. Well, that wasn't true. That remark on the radio when she'd said she was going to step out of the car to walk around in the daylight had been a piece of good news.

As long as she was even remotely as good as Agent Bill had been, he was golden. Her ability to walk in the sun would give his team a huge tactical advantage.

He left the command tent when he heard the SUV approach, and watched Eric get out of the driver's seat and step back to open the passenger door.

The woman who got out of the back seat was not what he was expecting. If he was at a fashion show, perhaps, but not here in the Florida Everglades, and he was even more surprised to see that Eric seemed to respect her. He didn't only treat her like a lady. Most of the guys who'd grown up in the South had manners like those. No, he treated her with respect—like he would a superior officer he got along with.

Shit, if he didn't watch his step, this woman would have all of his hardened men eating out of her hand. Well, if Eric and John were any indication, at least.

Now, if she could fight, his night might not be so bad. He went over to introduce himself.

## CHAPTER 9

**Everglades, FL, USA**

Bethany Anne appreciated Eric opening her door. He did it because he wanted to, not because it was the proper and required way to act. It touched her and made a very deep impression.

She saw the Agent-In-Charge come out of the tent and waited for him to come to her. She didn't know for sure what he was thinking, but she had a good idea. After the stories Eric and John had shared, she knew the agents from her agency had been accepted as a tactical expedient. It wasn't until Bill died, no replacement appeared, and the massive number of injuries and deaths had occurred on ops that it became obvious they were overmatched without help.

So, she understood this agent was hurting not only from the deaths in his group but also his pride. He had to wonder if she would be an asset or a prima donna pain-in-the-ass problem.

She hated not walking over to him but making him come to her set the right precedent.

He reached them and put out his hand to shake. "Agent Dan Bosse."

She returned his grip with the same amount of strength as

they shook hands. "Bethany Anne, Agent. I understand we have an infestation we need to get rid of quickly. How do you want to do this?"

Agent Bosse was flummoxed for a couple of seconds. He had expected the agent in front of him to be…well, not this, exactly. She was professional and polite and radiated capability. He had three decades on the teams, and he could tell she had been in the pit before. "Thank you, Agent Bethany Anne. Please come with me, and I'll get you up to date. I have your requested clothes as well." Dan turned and started walking back to the tent. If he didn't know better from people he trusted with his men's lives, he would not believe this woman was more than what she looked like—a sophisticated model.

By the end of the operation, Dan Bosse would know he never, ever wanted to piss this lady off. Then he would pray she would be the only agent he would have to work with for the rest of his career.

"Agent, it's just Bethany Anne. One name, no last name, and I am certainly not an agent."

Dan looked over his shoulder. "Oh?"

"Not like you're probably thinking, Agent Bosse. I'll help your team through the contacts you're familiar with, but I don't have the same position in the family Bill did before me."

They went into the large tent that was used as the operations center. Two laptops and a couple of large screens were set up to show weather radar on one and what looked like real-time satellite tasking on the other.

"If it isn't inappropriate, can I ask what your role in the family is?"

"It hasn't been formally quantified, Agent Bosse, but I'm confident that by the time I get to meet everyone, some will call me Bethany Anne and to others, I will be known as the 'Queen Bitch.'"

He smiled at her. "With affection?" Dan was trying to figure out when this meeting had gone off track.

"Oh, God, I hope not. If I don't have someone upset with me, then I'm not doing my job correctly."

Dan couldn't help himself. She had just provided more insight into the other side than Bill had in his whole career. "What job is that?"

This was the question Bethany Anne had worked the whole conversation to get to. "Agent Bosse, I'm here to crush the problems your team knows about, those you don't know about, and problems a thousand years in the making. If the supernaturals don't get their act in gear, they better find a priest. Most of these para-humans only understand strength and violence, and if there's one thing I'm good at, Dan…"

He was looking at that raven-haired beauty when her face lost the angelic look, and his hindbrain started freaking out in gibbering terror. He had been through a hundred operations and had seen Nosferatu and the two vampires from the family. He still occasionally woke up at night sweating from dreams related to the worst operations.

He became a believer when he saw the personification of destruction and torment looking at him with blood-red eyes and fangs sticking out of her mouth.

A deeper, malevolent voice finished, "…it's delivering violent messages. Any questions?"

Agent Dan Bosse just shook his head.

Her fangs retracted, and her eyes turned back to their natural color. She waited a few seconds for his heartbeat to settle down. "So tell me, who and what is the story behind the pricks who are the focus of the operation tonight?"

Agent Bosse had walked into the tent as a commander sharing information with someone who was at best a qualified support specialist. That changed. He proceeded to give the same presen-

QUEEN BITCH

tation he would give a powerful partner who had the ability to rain death and destruction on the enemy.

For the first time in ten years, he wished he could suit up and be on the sharp end, because the four agents going in with this woman would come out changed. He was sure their stories would become legend.

Dan cleared his throat and started by giving her the background. They had two Nosferatu, as far as they knew, holed up in the square mile of the Everglades he showed her on the map. They couldn't track them down to get to them during the day. Somehow, they protected themselves from the sun; the best guess was with mud. It had taken a while to get satellite tasking priority since it was only suspected that a couple of people had been eaten by alligators.

Then, a group of teenagers had been out having a drinking party. They claimed they saw a zombie kill a man fishing and drag him out into the water, where they both submerged, the man's body still kicking.

The news turned it into a story about an Everglades serial killer and their request for the satellite, which was on screen two, as well as eyes in the sky with incredibly sensitive FLIR cameras, suddenly became the priority. Tonight was their first opportunity to carry out the mission. The Florida State Police and State Guard were planning an operation through the Everglades in thirty-six hours. The preparation was in progress, and the news was focused on that operation. The government was trying hard to let the populace know something was being done about the serial killer.

They needed to get this solved quickly before it became a fustercluck.

Bethany Anne asked how they operated when Bill was with the team.

He explained that normally, Bill would take point and the rest of the team helped with support. Basically, if anything got around

Bill, they would try to kill it, contain it, or turn it back to Bill, who would then kill it.

"Okay, I get it. I'm the point. My job is to take down the baddies, and my team's responsibility is to help watch my back while I do it. If I get overwhelmed, they do what?"

"Well, we haven't had too many issues with that happening—yet. Unfortunately, Bill's last encounter was the one that told us the bad things had escalated. Generally, the team has a point person, and you'll need to work out the details with him."

"Who will be my point person?"

"John Grimes. He picked you up earlier."

"Oh."

"I had John and Eric pick you up to get a read on you. You were an unknown, and they had to get a relationship, whatever it could be, resolved as quickly as possible. I have to admit I'm surprised you bonded so rapidly. Bill would talk to the team members when they first got introduced, but over time he became quieter, just coming in, doing the op, and leaving. That reminds me; you don't have a Carl equivalent?"

"No. Carl is missing, if you didn't know that. I'm hoping we don't have to get too technically advanced." She pointed at the monitors showing the weather, spy, and FLIR information with her eyes. "I think you have it covered at the moment."

He looked at the setup. While it seemed pretty advanced, especially with the Everglades as the backdrop, he would have felt more comfortable with Carl's equipment and skills to back them up. He sighed.

"I hope so. It's been hell since Bill got taken down. I keep wondering when the other shoe is going to drop."

"What do you mean?"

Dan's face grew pensive. "I think Bill's attack was just the opening move. Our ops have been more frequent and more dangerous since that happened. Here, let me show you something." He turned to the agent behind the monitors. "Barry, would you pull up the maps with the operation locations on them?"

They moved behind Barry, looking over his shoulder as he pulled up a mapping program on the left monitor. The locations started in Northern California and continued throughout the Southwest and Midwest, finally stopping in Florida.

Bethany Anne grunted. "Huh, can't take the show into the Atlantic. So this is a big one, or they'll turn and go up the coast."

"That's what I'm thinking. It's one of the reasons I was relieved to get someone from your group. If this is going to be bad, I'm going to need all the help I can get."

"How have you set up the play?" She looked at Dan, getting a sense of his emotions as well as his logic.

"With you, I figure a five-person team. You, plus a group of four. Grimes, Escobar, English, and Jackson. I have an additional six shooters here with me, and I've got medics. I've added a second medic because of injuries we've taken."

"Okay, where's my gear? I'll get suited up. We have some daylight left, and I want to get ahead. Maybe we'll get lucky."

Dan yelled, "Grimes!"

John left the group of three men he was talking to, finishing the rest of his instructions to them. "...see that I don't. I'll bet you $500 I get off clean. You in?" Eric was the only one who declined the bet.

"Can you get Agent... Can you get Bethany Anne her gear? If she says she checks out on something and wants it, see if we have it in the weapons locker."

John kept his face carefully blank. "I'll do that, sir." John had previously sensed a frosty attitude for the vampire contacts from Agent Bosse. He seemed to be thawing around this one. Well, she'd made *him* comfortable with her in one car ride, so he was only a little surprised she was able to work with their commander.

MICHAEL ANDERLE

Dan left the tent, heading for one of the white cargo vans that served as a separate command area.

John walked over to Bethany Anne, ready to set the right tone. He smiled at her and said in a loud voice that carried well outside the tent, "Hey, fuckface, what kind of guns do you want?"

The sudden stunned silence was louder than a shout.

Bethany Anne looked up at John, who smiled down at her. She gave as good as she got. "Listen, gutter-ass, you had better do better than 'fuckface' when you try that or I'll make you get down and give me fifty, with me standing on your back. You feel me?"

John stopped smiling, but the sparkle was still in his eye. "Yes, ma'am. Just how heavy are you?"

Bethany Anne shook her head. "Don't you know never to ask a lady what she weighs? Shit, John, if you can't cope with simple social rules, I'm not sure you're going to work too well out in the 'Glades. Wait, never mind. Out there, I need muscle and testosterone. You're good for that much, right?"

John started with, "Lady..." but he saw Bethany Anne's eyes narrow. "I mean, yes ma'am!"

She smiled and said in a quiet voice, "Good. Now you better give me half that score with those two newbies out there, or I'll yank your dick up through your throat. Got that?"

John swallowed. "Uh, yeah. I got that, Bethany Anne." He pulled the box with her combat fatigues from behind the table. He still couldn't completely wipe the smile from his face as he exited the tent. The fire team's faces, except for Eric's, were *priceless*.

---

The Everglades had a musty smell, occasionally enhanced—if you could call it that—by stagnant water. Bethany Anne hoped she could smell the Nosferatu before they woke up. It was late in the afternoon, and they had covered the search area pretty well. For a while, they were able to use a couple of Jon boats. Then they'd found a sizable mound and poked and prodded into all sorts of nasty areas.

Before the team left, Bethany Anne had introduced herself to them. John and Eric she already knew, and that went a long way toward reducing the trepidation Scott English and Darryl Jackson felt.

Agent Scott English was an ex-NYPD SWAT team member. At 5'10" he was the shortest, but his chest was massive, and his arms must surely have been illegal in three states. He had been part of a particularly nasty event in Staten Island three years before. The SWAT team was called into what they thought was a hostage situation on the fourth floor of a tenement just after 10:00 pm. The bottom two floors had been evacuated, but the team had found blood all over the third floor and could hear screams on the fourth as they made their way up the stairs on both sides of the building. They were unprepared for the carnage and gruesome situation at the top.

One violent thirty-two-year-old stockbroker, a black male, had literally started ripping people apart and biting them at about 9:30 pm that night. The cops were called. They found the perp eating a small girl on the fourth-floor landing. Even after emptying their sidearms into David Aldwabi, he was able to grab the first officer, Lieutenant Matt Sanchez, a nine-year veteran. The stockbroker overpowered him easily, and Sanchez was killed. He bit through Sanchez's neck while he screamed in pain and held him while he bled to death. His partner, Sergeant Anthony Roberts, was able to call for backup before being killed by Aldwabi when he tried to help his partner. The perpetrator was too fast for Roberts, and as he tried to backpedal, he tripped over a dismembered arm. The attacker quickly broke his neck.

Scott and his team found Aldwabi cradling Roberts and patting his head slowly, staring vacantly into the distance. Unfortunately, Scott's team leader yelled at him to "Freeze." All that accomplished was to snap the man out of his unfocused state, and the screaming and gunfire began. Aldwabi was finally killed when the combined firepower of four SWAT rifles pulverized his chest and head. Scott's team leader lost his left eye and ear because he followed protocol with a Nosferatu.

The other guy, Darryl Jackson, was a black ex-Special Forces recruit. Darryl had joined the team six months ago to fill one of the unprecedented number of openings. Agent Bosse had contacted Frank to help him recruit, and he'd located Darryl working in the Pit overseas. He was coming up on his third rotation, and before he signed up again, Frank was able to convince him that his special skills could in fact be used in the United States to protect the innocent.

Darryl had thought he'd seen the worst with ISIS and how they beheaded those in the cities and towns they captured. Their reign of terror had nothing on the Nosferatu.

He had been in three operations so far, in Alabama, Louisiana, and Oklahoma. No one was sure why they'd skipped Texas.

Darryl had never been on an op with one of the good vampires—good being relative if you didn't presume it was equivalent to dead.

He did try to keep an open mind. Unlike the stories he had heard about Bill, this one was both talkative and hot to look at. Bill, on the other hand, was said to have been large, quiet, and usually, destructive as hell.

Unfortunately, Bethany Anne seemed a little small. Darryl wasn't too sure she would cut it.

Bethany Anne was staring into the distance when she heard the high keening behind her.

Darryl had apparently awoken a Nosferatu who had been hiding in a pile of detritus and rotting vegetation. By the time he had jumped back and thrown the stick to his side to grab his AR-15 in its quick-sling, his ears rang with the reports from Bethany Anne's .45s.

Generally speaking, most vets agreed there no pistol inflicted enough terminal damage ability to stop a determined opponent. The 9mm rounds were universally castigated by the men and women in the sandpit, and the Army had been looking to replace their M9s.

Regardless, Bethany Anne was able to squeeze off her shots fast enough to make it sound like an automatic. While Darryl's ears continued to ring, she stopped shooting, holstered her right pistol, and reached into the mess to pull out a very disgusting human-looking body. Half the head was blown off, and one eye socket leaked fluid. Holstering her other gun, Bethany Anne took out her MKIII knife and cut off the head quickly.

Darryl stared at her, amazed by the death and destruction he'd witnessed in the few seconds since he first uncovered the Nosferatu. All his concerns were completely forgotten.

She casually tossed the head fifteen feet away. "Stupid leg-humping cock-splurt wiper. Why did you scream like a little girl?" Her smile lit her face, and she quickly reloaded her pistols and policed her brass.

He couldn't help it. He busted out laughing at her cussing and got his shit back together. He had heard about her filthy mouth, so he decided to try his hand at giving as good as he got.

The rest of the team laughed when Darryl had to pump ten pushups while Bethany Anne stood on his back. She made him think of a unique curse word every time he rose up. She would have had him do fifty, but they needed to get back to it, and she felt it was enough to work the adrenaline through their systems.

During Darryl's pushups, John had given command ops an update on what happened. Bethany Anne hadn't paid too much attention to the radio, so she reached down and put the earphone in her left ear. They stayed a little closer as a group over the next half hour and tried to make sure no one was far from an easily accessible support person. When the sun officially slid over the horizon and it was getting dark, they pulled together, letting Bethany Anne have the lead position.

Two things happened at the same time. Another Nosferatu burst up off the ground about thirty-five yards to her right, and she could hear talk back in the ops center from the drone, warning that they had twelve rapidly approaching tangos coming at the ops center.

Agent Bosse had been right. They were in the middle of an ambush, and their help was miles away.

---

Back in the command ops van, Dan thought he wouldn't outlive his regret for not being better prepared.

---

Bethany Anne realized the base would be screwed if she didn't get back there. She had the new Nosferatu to take care of, however, and it had just gone into the water.

Fuck.

Agent John Grimes hated command decisions like this. He had three other agents for what he hoped was one Nosferatu. The guys back at the camp needed Bethany Anne.

"*Go!*"

Bethany Anne stopped peering at the water to try to predict where the Nosferatu was hiding and looked at John.

He had only seen Bethany Anne in fun moments, or at least non-stressful situations. The woman looking back at him with red eyes and glistening fangs made him start for a second. Realizing there was intelligence behind the feral face, he told her again, "Go! We got this one wanking spunk-butler. Help the team back at ops!"

Bethany Anne grinned at him—a weird situation when you

had fangs, he decided—and suddenly disappeared. "Holy shit!" The other men were professional enough to continue watching their quarters and ignored his outburst.

"Okay, guys, let's take this one down so she can take care of business."

Eric finished the thought. "Yeah, four of us against one Nosferatu. Bethany Anne against twelve Nosferatu. Seems fair."

"Well," Scott added, "we wouldn't want her to think we gave her the easier task because she's a girl, right?"

Darryl merely grinned. "I wouldn't let her hear you say that."

"*Fuck*, no!"

They all laughed at that response.

## CHAPTER 10

**Everglades, FL, USA**

Bethany Anne arrived on the docks where she had originally boarded her boat. It was the safest place to transport to, she reasoned.

The command ops area was a battlefield. She could see two Nosferatu with so many holes in them that they should be down. One agent was dragged, screaming, back toward the weeds behind the tent, and the cargo van had four supernaturals beating on it.

She decided to get their attention. Calmly, she pulled her 45s and shot each Nosferatu in the head.

"Come. Try. Me. You. Eye. Less. Ass. Bashers." Her words punctuated each shot. That was actually a pretty poor cussing effort, she decided. Good thing no one heard her.

*TOM, how much energy?*

**The portaling took a little over half your energy.**

Gott Verdammt! *I can't suck energy out of these creatures, can I?*

**Well, as a last resort, probably. Their nanocytes might cause you problems we don't need right now.**

*You got that fucking right.*

Bethany Anne went into super-speed and raced after the Nosferatu she had seen pulling the agent away. Eight of them from all over the camp tried to catch her while she went after him.

This would be a challenge. Without breaking her stride, she jumped into the air and shot two of them, emptying her pistols, and twisted around before landing.

At the corner, she could see the Nosferatu looking over his shoulder. The moment it realized she was coming for it, it dropped the agent's leg and turned toward her.

It wasn't even a contest. Bethany Anne holstered her right pistol and grabbed her knife. She impaled the creature in the skull and used the knife to twist its head around as she ran past. The Nosferatu dropped to the ground like a rag doll.

*Five down, six behind me, one missing, and my guys have another. Shit.*

She hoped she could take them all, but she didn't have a handy werewolf to grab and drink from. Well, shit, she hoped werewolf blood wasn't an acquired taste. Was it only a few weeks ago that even the thought of drinking blood made her queasy? Now, she joked about it while she ran from six Nosferatu.

Honestly, the running pissed her off. She finally spotted a sapling with a three-inch diameter trunk. That was perfect.

She raced past the tree, punching it hard. It shattered and dropped, but she kept a hard pace to increase the distance a little. She needed them to follow her. Finally, she stopped and turned. She was about a mile from the tree. Waiting for the ravenous horde of Nosferatu, she stood there with her thumbs tucked into her belt. As they drew close, she raised her right hand and gave them the finger. Then, she disappeared.

The Nosferatu keened in frustration. They ripped at the ground, trying to find a scent. Twenty seconds later, all hell broke loose when Bethany Anne, her eyes glowing red, ran back

MICHAEL ANDERLE

on the same trail they had just come from with a seven-foot-long, three-inch-diameter pole and tore into them. Her first swing took two Nosferatu heads. They exploded in gore.

The tree was almost wrenched from her hands when it connected with the supernaturals. It felt really good to get her mad on. It was four against one now, and she tossed the tree straight up ten feet, pulled her reloaded pistols, and shot two of them in their heads. It took a split second to re-holster her now empty pistols and catch the tree as it came down. Grabbing it like a spear, she threw it into the chest of the Nosferatu on her right. Running at the last one, she dropped, slid under it, and grabbed its legs. It fell face first into the mud. She turned and jumped, kneeing the creature in its head and crushing it, spilling brain matter all over her right leg.

*Gah, that was disgusting.*

The impaled Nosferatu tried to pull the tree out of its chest while Bethany Anne reloaded the last of her ammo. Calmly, she walked up to the struggling creature and blasted it into oblivion.

She had one fully loaded pistol and one with only three rounds. Checking with TOM didn't give her a good indication on how much energy she had left so she couldn't teleport back to the command base through the Etheric. Instead, she ran, putting everything she had into it.

Where was that last Nosferatu?

---

John was second-guessing his decision to let Bethany Anne leave. The one Nosferatu had somehow turned into two, and they were playing with John and his team.

They were completely screwed.

That was when Eric upped the ante. "Come get me, you ginormous shit-eater! Hey, spanky love-nuts and your friend fudge-slapper maximus over there!"

The men grinned. Bethany Anne wasn't there, but Eric was surely channeling her spirit. The men gripped their rifles and closed any gaps.

They might go down, but dammit, they would go down as her team, not as a group of 'Stupid leg-humping cock-splurt wipers.'

John took command. "On the count of three, Scott, I want you to keep fucktard number one over in the bushes busy. Eric, you and Darryl turn and let's try to light up fuck-nut number two over here. If we can get one down, we increase our chances of living a million percent."

"One…two…three!"

Bethany Anne heard the staccato burst of gunfire shatter the quiet as she ran back to the command center. Her team—her men—were in a battle. She feared she knew where the final Nosferatu had ended up.

*Gott Verdammt!* She raced to the campsite, trying to figure out a way to get to them. The Jon boats were not only too slow to help her reach them in time. They weren't even at the ops center anyway. They were still out in the Everglades.

Coming into the camp, she could see the men in defensive positions. One of them started firing at her unexpected appearance, assuming anything arriving suddenly wasn't human. It took a second for him to hear the cease-fire and by then, she had moved thirty yards away.

She found the man she was looking for, one of the two medics Agent Bosse had mentioned. Looking like a horror show with all the blood, guts, and brains on her plus the intensity of her gaze as she feared for her team, it wasn't a surprise the medic was speechless. "Do you have any bagged blood?"

He merely continued to stare.

"Look, snap out of it! Where is the blood? My team needs it!" Okay, technically, she needed it to help her team, but the guy didn't seem like clarification would help him right then. He turned and pointed back to a van next to the bigger cargo van.

"Over there, white insulated box. You can find it behind..." He realized she had already gone, shook off his confusion, and went back to helping Agent Flores who lay on a table before him.

Bethany Anne ripped the van door off, grabbed the chest, and put it on the ground. She opened the lid and pulled three packages of blood. Ignoring the people around her, she ripped the first bag open and drank. When she finished it, she threw it on the ground and started on the second. She was halfway done with it when she stunned the people watching her as she disappeared.

### **Everglades, FL, USA**

The fight was violent. The men had wounded the second Nosferatu, but it allowed the one Scott was trying to distract to almost reach them before the men pulled together again.

The Nosferatu, an old geezer when he'd been alive but considerably more mobile and dangerous now that he had changed, feinted left and rushed off to the right. Darryl was unable to get a bead on him, and he cut across, pushing Darryl back into Eric behind him and grabbing John who tried to get his gun on target.

The Nosferatu grabbed his gun arm with both hands and broke it. Then he backhanded him with his right hand, causing him to lose focus, then grabbed John's knife and stabbed him hard. He landed over ten feet away.

Though he no longer had John to worry about, the Nosferatu didn't have a chance when all three of the team opened fire. The creature jerked as bullets slammed into him and finally lost his footing and flew back onto the ground. Scott walked up and fired his pistol repeatedly, demolishing his head.

Eric told the other two to finish off the first Nosferatu and hurried to John. The knife was deeply embedded in his right pectoral.

"John, I got to tell you, no more tattoos on your chest—they won't look good with the scar you're gonna have."

John moaned and looked at him. His every breath wheezed as the knife had pierced his lung. They didn't have anything out there to help him, and he wouldn't make it back to the command center. "Have I told you you're a real prick lately?"

Eric grinned. "What did Bethany Anne tell you about lousy cussing, huh? She'll make you do fifty pushups."

John looked over Eric's shoulder and smiled a little. "I don't know, why don't we ask the little rectal-hole dictator herself?"

Eric turned around to see a thoroughly begrimed Bethany Anne behind him holding two bags of blood, one full and one only half full. She smiled at John. "So, you have to almost die to finally get the point, is that it, John?" She knelt beside him.

"Yeah, that white light has a way of focusing your creativity." He coughed hard.

"Do you trust me, John? I can heal you, but I can't explain. We don't have time. Will you trust me?"

He looked up at her and realized he wasn't looking into a monster's eyes but rather at hope, compassion, and concern wrapped in a package of blood and guts and the smell of gunpowder.

Scott and Darryl kept watch over the area. You could hardly see farther than ten feet without the flashlights.

It was eerily quiet.

John nodded. Bethany Anne grabbed the knife in his chest. "I'm going to pull out the knife, cut my wrist, and you have to suck as much of my blood as you can, do you understand me?"

John didn't open his eyes but nodded again.

Bethany Anne looked at Eric. "I need you to uncover that wound. Get the vest and his shirt ripped or anything you can do to access it while he's taking my blood."

Eric nodded. "Will he turn into a vampire?" He voiced the concern all the men had.

"No. My blood will heal him. It would take a bunch more to turn him. Enough talk, let's get ready."

On the count of three, she pulled the knife from his chest, slit her wrist, and, as he gasped in pain, stuck the wrist to his mouth, reminding him to suck on it. She had to cut it twice more because it kept healing on her.

Eric was able to lift the vest off the wound and cut away his shirt with his own knife. John stopped sucking on her wrist and dropped his head back down and to the side. Some of her blood dripped back out of his mouth.

"*Gott Verdammt*, John, that shit is priceless!" Bethany Anne slit her wrist one more time and let it drip into the hole in his chest, forcing it down with her finger. She lay back, willing it to work faster, then grabbed the full bag and drank it. The half-full bag had fallen over and spilled on the ground.

A little overcome with the fighting, teleporting, and now bloodletting, she lay back for a moment to close her eyes.

Darryl, Eric, and Scott had pulled out their flashlights, and two pointed out into the Everglades. Eric watched in fascination as Bethany Anne's fangs disappeared while she slept and then as the knife wound in his best friend and their team's leader closed up right in front of his eyes.

Scott had been talking to the guys back in the ops center. It was still a major mess over there. Agent Bosse had contacted Frank who had inbound medical support and additional agency support for cleanup. No one at the little island knew what to tell them yet about John. If anyone found out what had gone on and John died, they feared what might happen to Bethany Anne. They decided to say they were getting John prepped and would be back in thirty minutes.

Fifteen minutes later, John opened his eyes. He closed them quickly as Eric pointed his flashlight at him. "Dammit, Eric. Shine that light out there where the bad guys are, for fuck's sake."

"Good to hear your voice, you pain-in-the-ass." Eric smiled, but he moved the light to shine out into the Everglades. "Wouldn't want an alligator smelling all the blood and come for the buffet."

"What happened?"

Eric continued to talk as he trained his attention on the undergrowth outside their circle. "From when? When did you black out?"

John rubbed his chin with a finger. "Did I really drink blood from Bethany Anne? Am I going vampy, guys?"

"Yes and no. She promised it would only heal you. She said you had to drink a lot more to become a vampire. Although considering her upgrades, it might be worth it!" Scott and Darryl agreed as they maintained a tense watch, looking out into the night.

John stretched out his left arm and hit Bethany Anne's vest, right where her left breast was.

She spoke calmly into the night, keeping her eyes closed. "I just spent a lot of effort to heal you, Mr. Grimes. If you don't get your hand off my tit, I'm going to waste all of that effort when I kill you myself."

John moved his hand and chuckled. "Well, what do I spend the points on if not to buy a quick feel?"

Not wanting to banter right then, Bethany Anne merely said with exasperation, "John, I have a headache."

All the men laughed. Realizing what she'd said, she joined in. John finally summoned enough energy to slide his vest back on. "God, Bethany Anne, couldn't you have at least taken my shirt off nicely?"

From the ground, she replied, "John, you munchy butt-lover, it was Eric who wanted you so bad he ripped it off."

Eric looked at him and made kissing noises. The laughing started again. The two rested for another five minutes before she stood, reaching down to pull the massive Agent John Grimes up without showing the least amount of strain. She cocked her head.

"Incoming helicopter. Let's try to look like we're professional, men."

Within sixty seconds, a black Marine Venom flew in. It landed a hundred feet away, and two marines with flashlights on their weapons jumped out. The four men created a circle around Bethany Anne.

There was no way they would let any misunderstandings occur on their watch. She might look like the monster hell had kicked out, but this vampire, by God, was *their* vampire.

They scrambled into the chopper, the two marines the last on, and one gave the signal. The black Venom turned the lights off and lifted into the air, heading toward the ops center.

CHAPTER 11

**Everglades, FL, USA**
Agent Dan Bosse counted his lucky stars, which were plentiful in the sky above the Everglades. This far from any major metropolitan area, the light pollution was about zero. He had needed a minute to get out of his post-attack funk.

A Marine Venom helicopter approached, turning its lights on and ruining his beautiful night view, so he turned and walked back to the camp.

There was a bunch to be thankful for. This could have been a monumental disaster. He had over twenty people on this op and everyone—including himself—would have been killed this evening had it not been for Bethany Anne.

Dan had no idea what she'd done, exactly. Apparently, within a minute after the Nosferatu attacked, she had appeared and shot every single one. She hadn't killed any of them but ran after one of his agents who was dragged away. They'd found him about fifty yards behind the command tent. He would survive. They'd also found two Nosferatu with their heads almost obliterated by huge bullet wounds. Another's head had been twisted around, and a large knife wound gaped in the forehead.

An easily followed path led eastward out of the camp. A mile or so outside, they'd found a tree stump and a bunch of limbs. Two miles further, they had discovered six more Nosferatu. Two had no head, and two had their heads destroyed by bullets. One lay with its face in a large depression in the ground like a war hammer had hit it, and a final Nosferatu had a large sapling sticking up out of it with most of its head shattered by bullets.

According to the story doing the rounds, she had shown up and demanded blood from a medic, ripped off his van door, grabbed some, and drank it. Then she'd disappeared again. Shortly after, a shootout took place between Agent Grimes' group and…something. The men had been cagey over the radio, Dan wasn't quite sure what went down.

Back at the ops center, he watched as the helicopter landed about thirty-five yards away. John and Scott were the first two off, then Bethany Anne, and finally, Eric and Darryl. They seemed to provide a security cordon around her, though he had no idea why until they got closer.

Bethany Anne looked tired. Exhausted, actually. She was also covered in blood and filth. He had barely heard her voice over the noise of the helicopter earlier. "And if you ever touch my tit again, John, I will kick your nads from here to Miami. Are we clear?"

Dan looked up. John's vest was badly damaged, and he had blood all over his chest, but he looked the freshest of them all. Like he'd just had a full night's sleep and a great breakfast. Yup, there was a story there.

"Yes, ma'am."

The men let their rifles hang on their quick-slings. John approached Dan. "Team Queen Bitch reporting in." He grabbed his ear, yelped in pain, and turned around to look at Bethany Anne. She merely pointed at Scott who rolled his eyes.

Somehow—and he would have to figure out how—this woman had not only saved his command, helped kill at least fourteen Nosferatu, but had also brought her team back alive. Regardless of the blood and damage to John's chest, everyone seemed in good health and spirits. Dan shook his head.

Some other time. He wouldn't ruin anything with this woman tonight.


### New York City, NY, USA

Nathan let Ecaterina sleep in as she was a little jetlagged. He left some bananas and apple juice on the counter for her.

He didn't feel the effects of time changes when traveling as she did. Having done it a lot in his life, it was no longer a big deal. Taking care of business, he left messages for both Frank and Gerry.

That done, he picked up more food from the corner store and carried the two bags of groceries home. He went a little heavy on the fruits and nuts. While he could call in for delivery of the major meals until they worked something out, he knew Ecaterina liked to snack on 'real food,' so he got plenty.

Once he'd dropped the food off in the kitchen, he went up to the second floor to catch up with the backlog of work for his security company and the other miscellaneous businesses he was involved in. He went through all the local companies first. They'd never caused any problems in the past, and that was true this time as well. He made sure nothing in the finances for the real estate concern looked fishy and closed that bank account window. He had scheduled a 10:30 meeting with the two managers at his security agency, and that was in only a few minutes.

Nathan took the time to pull a fresh t-shirt and dress shirt on but retained his shorts. It had been brisk outside, but the temperature inside was pleasant. With a jacket, he could avoid getting too dressed up. New York City had a few days of snow a week before, but it had apparently melted almost as fast as it had fallen.

He had requested a Skype call with his staff, so they couldn't see lower than his shirt, anyway.

At 10:30, he called the first, and once he had him online, conferenced in the second.

He asked about the Guardian project, and both relayed that they were thankful for the help in implementing it across all their clients so fast. They could have had a bad time otherwise. Nathan was happy with that. Frank had bribed him with as many prime network guys as he needed if he would discover Michael and Bethany Anne's whereabouts. He had jumped at the offer. While Nathan was a world-class hacker, he couldn't do the same job as a bunch of incredibly competent network admins working simultaneously. It was a pretty easy decision to take Frank up on the bribe.

Since going to Europe, he had met and almost died for Ecaterina—the lady who, right now, slept downstairs. He sighed. He knew she would go with Bethany Anne when she got back, but he hoped the vampire might stay away for a few more days. Maybe a couple of weeks? Or, if he was devious, he could hack her airline reservations and keep changing them.

He grinned. To keep Ecaterina around, he would do that to anybody in an instant. Except for Bethany Anne. One, she would certainly find out. He had never learned how she knew one of his hacker personas. Two, when she found out, life would be incredibly painful. He didn't know exactly how, but he did know she could be really creative when she inflicted suffering.

Either way, Ecaterina was connected to her, and he was bound up with Ecaterina, for sure.

His ears picked up that the lady in question had just gotten out of bed. A couple of minutes later, he heard the shower start. He decided he would go upstairs and take another quick shower himself. While he hadn't sweated much that morning, he wouldn't take a chance.

Ten minutes later, he came down dressed in jeans, a T-shirt, and a sweater and carrying a black leather jacket for his trip to see Gerry.

He caught Ecaterina digging through the fresh fruits and eating an apple. She smiled at him and covered her mouth with her hand as she chewed.

"Good morning, Nathan."

"A good morning to you too, sleepyhead."

She pursed her lips. "What is this sleepyhead? Is my hair messed up? I brushed it after my shower." She patted her hair and turned to see if she could see anything in the reflection of the double oven.

"No, Ecaterina. It means someone who was sleepy, who slept a long time."

"Oh, so you think to already start on criticizing me on my first day here in America?" Her face became a picture of righteous indignation.

*Oh, shit,* he thought. How did a woman turn the tables in a second language so quickly?

He wrestled with what to say when she suddenly smiled and said, "Gotcha, Mr. Lowell," and bit into the apple again.

He grinned. Man, it felt so good to be off the hook! He had forgotten the downsides to a relationship. The reality was that women had so many cards they could play, it was maddening.

Then he drank in her smile and knew it didn't matter to him. He would take it all.

"Before you get too far into that apple, would you like to have lunch? I have a meeting with Gerry you can come too, or not. Whatever you want to do."

She looked down at the mostly eaten apple, took the last two bites, and gave him a thumbs-up. On her way past him, she extended one finger, then went to her bedroom and shut the door. Since she wore shorts, he was not complaining.

Barely a minute later, she emerged dressed for cool weather in a white jacket, blue shirt, jeans, and tennis shoes of a brand he didn't recognize. He supposed they were European. He would see if she liked Puma, one of his favorites.

"Ready!" A lady who took only one minute to change? Priceless.

He didn't want to do any driving, so he had called a taxi while she was changing.

They sat and talked about different foods she might like to try while waiting for the taxi to show up. By the time they had decided on New York pizza, the cab had arrived. He had to explain to her that New York pizza would *not* be like anything in Italy or even similar to the pizza true Italians made.

She was game. If it was pizza, she could get excited about it.

He decided to start with Joe's Pizza in the West Village; they had the foundational New York pizza. It was universally agreed that if someone was new in town, you took them to Joe's. Traffic slowed the trip considerably, and the apple from breakfast hadn't lasted very long for her. She was hungry again.

They finally got to Joe's, and he paid the cab fare. The pizza joint was little more than a hole in the wall in a brown-brick building with a lot of outside fire escapes running up the building and a big white sign with Joe's Pizza on it. The word Joe's was in script. Beneath the sign was a red overhang with a walk-up white marble bar on the right side of the door. A 24-hour ATM sign adorned the left side. Inside, the room was narrow and long with the pizza counter in the back past a few stand-up tables. The drinks were displayed in a self-serve stand-up cooler. They were so proud of the fact Joe's was shown in the movie *Spider-Man* that they had it plastered on their hanging sign on the wall. On the other side were the customary pictures of famous and not-so-famous people enjoying themselves at Joe's.

While New York was significantly dirtier than Brasov, Ecaterina didn't seem to mind. A couple of times, he noticed she wrinkled her nose. He could understand that. Still, he appreciated that she didn't let a couple of things she didn't like ruin her experience.

They reached the counter, and both ordered the two-slice-and-a-drink option. After taking her to a table, he got to enjoy her eyes light up with pleasure as the deliciousness that was Joe's played like a violin in her mouth.

He bit down on his pepperoni slice. God, he thought, it was so good to be back home.

He smiled. He was thinking, *Hey, Ma, look what I brought back from Romania. Can I keep her?* His mom had passed away many years back, but he thought she would approve.

They finished their pizza and spent some time walking around. Finally, he hailed a cab and gave the driver Gerry's address.

It took too long and yet didn't take long enough to reach Gerry's building. He exited the cab and held the door for Ecaterina, then closed it behind her. He had paid for the cab with his credit card en route.

They walked into the building and up to the security podium. The guard took one look at Nathan and let him know he was good to go on up with a quick head bob. The security guard then did a double take at Ecaterina.

Nathan decided she deserved two looks. If the guard took a third, he would box his ears, though.

They stepped onto the elevator. It wasn't the speediest in New York but not the slowest, either. That might go to the elevator in the Prada store. He smiled, thinking he should get Bethany Anne over to the Prada store if she hadn't been there yet. She would love the fashion and then lose it when the elevator seemed like it was going nowhere fast. They even had curved benches for people to sit on and look through the glass to view the merchandise as the elevator crept ever so slowly from floor to floor.

The elevator dinged and they got out. He waved to Stacy at the reception desk who waved back and then suddenly stopped as she realized the gorgeous lady coming off the elevator was following Nathan. Then he stopped and made sure she caught up. Stacy was definitely in a funk.

Nathan knocked politely on the door before opening it. Gerry would have scented him coming down the hallway. The air vents had been specifically directed to point the airflow down the hall and into his office.

Sneaky bastard.

It had taken Nathan a couple of weeks to realize Gerry had designed a passive friend/foe detection system. He loved it. When one entered the office, his desk was twenty feet away. On the right were a couch, coffee table, and two chairs that faced the opposite wall. On the left was a large screen TV system and beneath that, some built-in cabinets. Behind the couch on the right was a little space to allow someone to access the bar. It was well stocked with different liquors. They were displayed with lights shining up through them as you would see at fancier bars and were very attractive. Gerry's desk had two chairs facing it with a small round table between them.

He got up from behind his desk to give Nathan a huge hug and a couple of slaps on the back. "It is so damned good to see you again. Do you have any idea what a pain in the ass those people under you are?"

Nathan merely looked at him, deadpan.

Gerry smiled. "Never mind, of course, you do!" He turned to Ecaterina. "My sincerest apologies, my lady. I didn't notice you when I saw my good friend show up. My name is Gerry."

Ecaterina reached to shake his hand and returned the introduction in her sexy Romanian accent. "Hello, Gerry, it is nice to meet you. My name is Ecaterina Romanov."

Gerry looked at Nathan, perplexed. Nathan thought maybe he was expecting someone else? Ah!

Nathan spoke up, "Gerry, Ecaterina is Bethany Anne's close friend and in her circle of trust. I brought her here to America because Bethany Anne wanted to have a conversation with Michael's child, Stephen, before returning herself. Ecaterina is staying with me."

When Nathan put the emphasis on 'staying with me,' Gerry knew he was really putting a claim on her. The guys in the pack had better treat her gently, or there would be hell to pay. That was only from Nathan. Gerry thought if Nathan didn't get enough of a pound of flesh—without blood—then Bethany Anne would forgo the no-blood requirement.

Since she knew Bethany Anne, Gerry had to ask, "Ecaterina. Are you aware of Nathan's, uh, peculiarities?"

"You mean that he turns into, what you call, friendly pooch?" Gerry saw Nathan wince at this description. Oh, Gerry intended to keep this description alive.

"Why, yes, that he turns into a 'friendly pooch' is exactly what I mean." Yup, Gerry could officially call it. Nathan was taken.

There would be ladies all over America unhappy with this relationship. Gerry had been shown a bulletin board where certain women had shared everything they knew about Nathan to try to figure out a way to hook him and reel him in. Gerry wondered how this one had done it so fast. Well, that would be a story for another time.

"Let's sit. Would you care for anything to drink, Ecaterina? Oh, yeah, Nathan, you too." Nathan didn't miss Gerry's huge smile. Oh well, it wasn't like he had seriously expected to hide his affection for Ecaterina.

But now, she had called his wolf a 'friendly pooch.' He wasn't sure if that was her lack of English skills, her deft handling of payback for the sleepyhead comment this morning, or something else.

CHAPTER 12

**New York City, NY, USA**
Nathan got along great with Gerry. Together, they had a working system. Gerry would stay in the top spot playing politics with everyone, and Nathan would make sure the pains in the asses in his personal pack didn't constantly annoy him. The fact that working with vampires was his main occupation had now turned around and bitten him in his own ass.

He watched Ecaterina shake Gerry's hand. Okay, so working with the newest vampire had benefits.

Then, she said he was a 'friendly pooch.' His carefully neutral face slipped a little. *Oh my God, did she just say that?*

He went through the horrible scenarios in his head. How many assholes would he have to deal with before he got through this mess? He wanted to rub his face in frustration, but Gerry looked at him with a huge smile. He decided not to give the guy another reason to gloat. Gerry asked him if he wanted something to drink.

What he wanted was two fingers of whiskey followed by three more, but he realized that was the frustration talking again. "Yeah, how about some water?"

## QUEEN BITCH

Grabbing two waters, Gerry gave one to Ecaterina and the other to Nathan, and while they sat in the chairs in front of his desk, he walked back around the huge thing and sat down. He looked at Nathan. "You have no idea how my life has sucked since you've been gone, my friend."

Nathan smiled, enjoying the appreciation. "Yeah, actually, I do." Okay, now he knew the negotiating edge he could use to make sure Ecaterina's little comment didn't go any further. Maybe the damage could be mitigated. "Let's get down to business without your 'woe is Gerry' venting for the next thirty minutes. What about the troublemakers here? Does the Council have any ideas?"

"Sadly, very few. Half of them want to wring their necks, while the other half feel the young need to vent their spleen and we should give them some time. They're too focused on the fact Michael has gone. So what are they going to do, kill their own?"

Nathan considered that. It was true the Pack Council handed out death sentences from time to time for heinous crimes against humanity. But not for merely talking smack. The vampires always handled the issue if they heard it in person. It was only when the pack talked outside the UnknownWorld and it got back to Michael's family that it became a problem. Of course, it almost always got back to Michael when Carl or someone filling his role was involved. Then, a vampire would start executions, and the first the Council would know about it was when they received frightened phone calls. Often, these calls came in the middle of the night from the spouses or significant others of the suddenly non-communicative werewolves who had lost their heads. Occasionally, even right next to them in bed. Scary as hell.

The problem was that the young had a really short attention span and believed they would live forever. "Gerry, if we don't get ahead of this problem, I'm afraid we'll have another Valentine's Day event."

Gerry knew Nathan wasn't pulling his leg, but he had a hard

time understanding the enormity of it. He didn't want to remember the details of that day. There had been so much blood, and that bastard Michael had actually played with a couple of his personal friends by ripping their arms off before pinning them to the floor and allowing them to...sort of grow together before doing it again.

Unfortunately, what had happened was exactly the sort of thing he had warned the Council about for five years before the slaughter happened. Gerry had felt like Noah must have in the Old Testament when everyone had laughed at him as the Ark door closed, only to have them screaming during the flood. He could have tried to fight, but it would have been pointless.

Someone would need to be available to pull the packs together to ensure this was the only retribution for the massive breach of Michael's honor the Council had instigated. Why so many of his fellow alphas thought they could take Michael down had always confused Gerry. Even most of the seconds and thirds behind the fools followed their leaders into calamity.

Well, they'd all followed that foolishness into death.

Two of the alphas had tried to sneak out through an airshaft they could barely fit into. Michael had pulled them both back out and simply cut their heads off with his hands. Gerry had watched but never understood. It was like Michael had wolverine hands, though Gerry never saw any knives or metal. Occasionally, as he had when those two tried to escape, he simply sliced and the blood sprayed everywhere while the head landed a few feet away, cut off cleanly.

But to be worried that a new vamp could do this? It made no sense.

Nathan continued. "I can see your doubt, my friend. And trust me, when I first saw her walk into the bushes where I fought Algerian and one of his lackeys, I saw red-eyed death. The other wolf jumped her. She caught him in the air. She didn't even stagger at the weight, Gerry. Then, she watched us both as she pulled the wolf's head almost completely off and drank his blood, which sprayed everywhere. Then she simply stepped over the body and told the two of us to change. I obeyed and that idiot Algerian decided he would go for my throat. He never had a chance. He had barely moved in my direction before she grabbed him, picked him up, and threw him down on the ground like it was nothing. He had to be at least twenty pounds heavier than me. Then she picked him up again and hit him on the back of the skull with her forearm to knock him out."

"Why did she knock him out?"

"Questioning. She wanted answers out of him. Which, by the way, she got. During the interrogation, she was waiting for Algerian to wake up. Somehow—I guess she heard his heartbeat or sensed something—she knew he had woken up and was playing possum. She went to the fire and grabbed a burning stick and told Alexi, a werebear, to hold him down. When he had a foot on him, she thrust the stick against his body. He stopped pretending he was asleep and struggled like hell to get away from the burning stick. She tells him to change back immediately or suffer again until she's satisfied he's learned the lesson. He decided to shift."

"Then what?"

"She got the information out of Algerian, but not before he tried to come after me again. She caught him, and this time, pinned his hand to the ground with my silver-laced Bowie knife. She warned him that the next time, it would be with a five-inch tree trunk. He got the message. When she had what she wanted, Alexi asked to finish the execution as it was personal. Even a thousand-pound werebear was on his best behavior around her. She might be young, but do not underestimate her, Gerry. That lady is death walking when she wants to be."

Gerry was still unconvinced, and Nathan called him on it.

"You don't seem to get it, Gerry. Don't. Underestimate. Her."

Gerry shook his head. "Nathan, I get it. I trust you're telling me the truth, but I have half the Council advocating strenuously to break from the strictures and the other half wringing their hands. None of Michael's kids are talking to Frank, which means no one expects them to come over to the new world to deal with anything. They will assume it's Bethany Anne's problem and the rebellion group sees a great opportunity to be free again."

Nathan pursed his lips. "Gerry, I'll tell you what. If you decide to either do nothing or, God forbid, support this idiocy, then let me know. I'll get Ecaterina and me two tickets back to Romania and wait until the dust settles. Hell, Alexi would let us run over his mountain, I bet."

Gerry's eyes hardened. He had known Nathan for a long time, but there he was, announcing his intention to leave if trouble erupted. He almost said something he would regret when he realized he could be looking at himself a hundred and fifty years before, trying to make the first Council understand that attacking Michael was death.

He shook his head, leaned back in his chair, and sighed. Ecaterina spoke up.

"I don't know why you two boys try to figure this out just by yourselves. Why don't you call Bethany Anne and ask her?"

Nathan wanted to slap his forehead, and Gerry looked surprised. "What? She'd talk to us about it?"

Nathan snorted. "Yeah. I didn't mention she wasn't going to kill Algerian because he was fighting. He merely didn't listen to her ultimatum. He signed his death sentence when he disobeyed *her*, not because he disobeyed something the strictures said. She doesn't always agree with Michael's rules. Ecaterina, here, is the first example. She didn't wipe any of the UnknownWorld from her mind."

Gerry turned his head and looked at her. "I was wondering…"

It was Ecaterina's turn to scoff. "Just like men. Snort and beat your breast when just talking might solve it." She reached into her white coat and pulled out her cell phone. Bethany Anne's speed dial went immediately to voicemail, so she left a message. "Hey, it's Ecaterina. Nathan has a small issue come up with the Weres and the Council, and he and—" she looked quickly at Gerry to get his permission, and he nodded, "Gerry need to talk to you about some idiocy with younger Weres. They need to know your opinion about something before all the stupid stuff starts. Give them or me a call. Hope it's going well with Stephen."

She hung up and stared at them. Nathan looked relieved, and Gerry looked confused.

"Stephen?"

She answered. "Yes, one of Michael's children who is based in Romania. She went to track him down and have—what did she call it, Nathan? It started with a 'd?'"

Nathan shook his head and smiled. "She called it a 'discussion,' but she used it as a euphemism. She went to lay down the law, and he would either get in line or she would kick his ass, and if that didn't work, she would take him out."

Gerry wanted more information about Stephen. Ecaterina didn't want them going down that road. That was Bethany Anne's personal business, and she didn't feel they needed to butt in.

"So, the word euphemism is when you use one word for another you don't want to say in polite company?"

"Yeah, that pretty much sums it up. Or you could use it as a joke, too."

"I still don't translate jokes that well in English, but I will get better. I promised Bethany Anne I would work on my English, so I need to understand this euphemism better. Can you two help me?" She smiled her best 'please, oh please' smile.

She looked expectantly at the two men who had totally forgotten their big argument from a minute before and now tried to upstage each other in explaining euphemisms.

Nathan started. "Here is an example—passed away instead of died."

Gerry came back with, "Correctional facility instead of jail."

"Letting someone go instead of fired." Nathan raised his eye at Gerry as if to say 'your turn.'

"Collateral damage instead of deaths."

Nathan gave a point to Gerry. "Big-boned instead of fat."

Gerry conceded a point to Nathan with his head. "Time-challenged instead of late."

Nathan held out his hand and twisted it left and right like, "not quite good enough." "Sanitation engineer instead of garbage man."

That got Gerry to award a point to Nathan. It was two points to one.

You merely needed the right bait, she thought. Plus, she was learning new things. Two birds, one stone.

### Washington, DC, USA

It was ten o'clock that night when Frank finally had a chance to talk to Agent Bosse alone. He had sent the Marines to help when the entire force came under attack. Both Frank and Bosse had been concerned about an ambush compromising the operation. It was the reason he had moved heaven and earth—or at least called in military favors—to get Bethany Anne to Florida in time.

He heard the story from Dan, his surprise growing as the facts unfolded. Bethany Anne was significantly more powerful than he had expected, even with Nathan's urging to take her seriously. She'd been picked up in Constanta, Romania, which meant she had probably met with Michael's child Stephen. He wondered how that went.

Dan explained that she had not only handled the Nosferatu at the base, but somehow, she'd managed to help her team who had taken out two on their own and in the open with no fatalities. He then went on to explain how their story definitely did not add up.

Frank wanted clarification on the team's story. "Why's that?"

He waited for Dan's explanation. "My main team lead is a guy by the name of John Grimes. She definitely made both him and his number one, Eric, comfortable before they even arrived. But something happened out on that little island in the 'Glades. When the five of them came off that chopper after the battle, the four team members surrounded her like she was a princess and they were the guards. Mind you, she was in black battle fatigues covered head to foot in mud, blood, and gore and looking like she couldn't lift a pencil off the floor. She was exhausted. Then John came up to me, and his vest was completely mangled. Had a big hole where a knife went through it, and he had blood all over his chest and a little on his neck and chin. All were covered in mud and stuff, but John's vest looked like he had been stabbed. But he was walking like he'd just woken up. She did something out there to heal John."

"So, what's your problem with that?"

"Frank, don't be an ass. I realize I've been a dick about vampires for fifteen years, and I own this one. She is one tough nut, and I mean that in a nice way. But what did she do out there? Will John stay human? Does she have some sort of connection with those men, something that can make them do what she wants? Get this—as they get off the helicopter, I hear the end of a conversation where she tells John he better not 'touch her tit again' or she would kick him in the privates all the way to Miami."

Dan sighed on the other side of the phone. "Look, Frank, I'm not freaking out, and I can't tell you about other vampires, but I'm good working with Bethany Anne. I merely don't like surprises, and now I have to reevaluate my vampire prejudice. Give me something that says I'm not being mind-melded or whatever. I want to know she's the real deal and isn't playing my men and me."

Frank thought about that. Could she? Actually, the bigger question was *would* she? He couldn't rule anything out with Bethany Anne since he didn't know much about her except the facts in her dossier. Every bit of information, including the two guys he had over in Romania tracking down the stories, helped him create a picture of her. Just this morning, he finally tracked down a Paul Rutherford who had gone to the police to give a statement and virtually vomited up all his crimes. They had tracked him back to the same train she and Nathan were on. One of his crimes included trying to use Rohypnol on women. Apparently, he found one woman it wouldn't work on.

"Dan, I don't have an easy answer for you. My gut feeling says no. She wasn't anything like that before she was transformed, and from my research, vampires don't change their core personality. In fact, it usually accentuates it. One of the biggest concerns I have is Bethany Anne going berserk if she met some stupid gang which either attacked her or some innocent bystander. She hated injustice before, and she won't allow it now."

"Why would her meeting a gang be a problem? They certainly wouldn't be able to hurt her. Hell, a few less gangbangers might be a good thing."

"Dan, I'm not worried about one or two. But if someone intelligent enough finds twenty gang members in different homes, all dead? When the deaths include people's arms and legs torn off, or heads splattered all over the place, I think we would find the FBI all up our asses, what do you think?"

Dan had almost lost a cousin to gangbangers. They'd thrown her violently out of the car when carjacking her new Camaro. "I think I wouldn't mourn their loss too much and I'd help hide the bodies."

*Okay,* Frank thought, *that was a bad example.*

"Frank, I hear what you're saying. We're trying to keep this out of the public eye, and a bunch of Feds with those big FBI letters on their jackets only draws the reporters. I get it. So you're telling me you think she's the real deal—what I see is what I get?"

"Pretty much. Oh, I'm not suggesting you stop being polite, but if she *is* easygoing, then I wouldn't think it's all a ruse to get you off balance and then kill someone."

"Hey, tell me what you think of this story."

"Okay."

"So, I talked to Bethany Anne in the command tent, and we finished up. Then, as I walked out, I told John Grimes to get her fatigues. As I walked away, I hear John—who was then in the tent with Bethany Anne—practically yell at her, 'Hey fuck-face, what kind of guns do you want?' Frank, you could have heard a pin drop it got so quiet. I thought he'd lost his ever-loving mind." Dan paused.

"So, tell me the rest!"

"She told him he had to do better than 'fuckface,' or she'd make him get down and do fifty pushups while she stood on top of him."

"Huh. Who would have thought a vampire had a good sense of humor? Well, that about confirms my guess that you have the real Bethany Anne with you. That being the case, I really would suggest a box of athletic cups for your men who don't know her well enough. If she thinks any of them are being sexist toward her, they might not find him again—ever. She put a few in the hospital, and that was before she was a vampire. Imagine what she can do now."

"No, I don't think she would get a chance to hurt anyone. These men love her. I think they would beat the shit out of anyone who didn't treat her right. That includes their best friends. It's kind of scary."

"So, we're seeing a real charismatic leader here, huh?"

"Yeah, that's about right."

"Good, that helps me with another problem. I need someone

to pick up the pieces on the American Council side. They're being a bunch of pussies on one side and breast-beating nutcases on the other. Gerry is trying to decide what to do. Fortunately, Nathan is back, and he's the Were who found Bethany Anne over in Romania. Well, maybe she found him…whatever. He met her in Romania and was supposed to talk to Gerry earlier today. I really hope they had a good conversation."

"Well, me too. Werewolves and the other Weres are nothing to sneeze at. I wish I had some on my team from time to time, but they keep telling me the rules won't allow it. They just wouldn't tell me whose rules."

"That was probably Michael's strictures. They wouldn't even admit that much because they fear him too much. That's part of the problem; they don't fear Bethany Anne enough."

Dan laughed. "Frank, if you saw what I did when her eyes glowed red and her fangs grew out of her mouth? Well, let's say you get religion pretty quickly."

"Good! That's good to know. Now, I just have to make a connection happen."

"Yeah, you worry about that, I'll worry about what I got down here. You need anything from Bethany Anne?"

"No, I'll call her directly if I do. No need to get you caught up in our conversation."

"Okay, thanks for the Marines; it was a boost there at the end. I'm going to see if she has anywhere to stay. If she doesn't, we'll get her a room with us to clean up and rest. Talk to you later."

"Bye." The line went dead.

Frank was tired. He had been up all day and monitored the takedown and the ambush as best he could. He needed to be more rested when he talked to Bethany Anne again.

He closed his office down and went home.

CHAPTER 13

**Florida City, FL, USA**
Bethany Anne washed her hair the next morning in her room at the Cambria Hotel in Florida City. It had six floors, and hers was on the fifth. She didn't care. The team had taken her in through the back. Even after the washout in the 'Glades, she was a complete mess. She'd reached her room, dropped her clothes, and taken a long, hot shower and scrubbed everywhere until her skin looked pink.

Then, she'd simply faded into the night on the bed. She finally got up when she couldn't take the sunlight through the window, having failed to close the drapes before she went to sleep.

Now, she felt better. The fight had been draining but not too bad. She needed to remember to keep blood on her when she went into battle— her own type of healing potion. She smiled at the thought. The problem with regular blood would be the limited amount of energy she could get from one bag and the type of protection she would need. If she could concentrate it into a smaller amount, maybe a vial, that would be perfect.

*TOM, have you got a moment?*
**Like I do much in here, Bethany Anne.**

*Give it a rest, TOM. I know you hit the computer from time to time.*

Uh, well, I'm just trying to get the connection going.

*You're doing an all right job. The headaches are only minor, and I appreciate that you leave me alone. It can't be too exciting to simply be a tagalong.*

Actually, Bethany Anne, quite the opposite. Your adventures so far have been fascinating and give me plenty to think about after they are over.

Bethany Anne thought back through everything that had happened since she turned. Maybe he had a point.

*Glad to hear it. Listen, can you work on a problem? I need to see if we can bottle the Etheric.*

You mean like the blood?

*Yes, only better. The amount of energy in a bag of blood is pretty substantial. But I can't carry ten bags of blood into a fight.*

What amount are you looking for?

She thought about that. They hadn't actually figured out what her max was, and only pulling from the Etheric was enough to reduce her need for food and water and provided a constant if small amount of extra. But the amount of energy expended during a battle was stupefying. If the medic hadn't been there with the extra blood, John would be dead right now.

*What about the same amount as twelve bags of blood, but something in a really small vial I can carry on my body?*

I'll see what I can do. It's a good suggestion, but I don't have any ideas at the moment. Can I use the computer for this?

Bethany Anne grimaced. Anytime he truly used the computer, her head hurt like a motherfucker.

*Yeah, hold on. Let me see if I can get some pain medicine up here first. We need to solve this problem. While you're picking around with the computer, see if you can figure out why it hurts me so much.*

I'll do that too.

QUEEN BITCH

Bethany Anne called down to the front desk and ordered up some pain relievers. She asked for a bottle and only grimaced a little at the cost. For a woman who had the wealth she had now, even the price of a Tesla was a rounding error.

Five minutes later, she received the medication and popped all twelve. What helped and what was too much, TOM could deal with.

She lay on the bed and waited for the pain.

TOM didn't disappoint. On the bad side, the first fifteen minutes hurt more than anything she had felt in months. After that, it became bearable, and somewhere around forty-five minutes into the process, she went to sleep.

An hour and a half later, she woke up and felt good.

*TOM, are you finished?*

**Hmm? What? No, why?**

*I don't feel any pain.*

**Oh, I found the problem and was able to fix it.**

*What was it?*

**What was what?**

His evasions roused her suspicious.

*What was the problem, TOM? Why did it hurt so much in the first place?*

**Well, there was a problem with the connections.**

*TOM, don't make me drag this out. What was the problem?*

**They were connected incorrectly.**

*So, you're saying you connected the computer to my mind wrong, right?*

This was way too confusing.

**Yes, I connected the computer incorrectly the first time. It took me about fifteen minutes to establish that and about thirty minutes to fix it. I'm sorry.**

Bethany Anne, relieved the computer was online and no longer caused her any pain, felt no annoyance at the mistake. It wasn't like TOM had a manual on how to connect Kurtherian organic computers to a human.

*Apology accepted.*

A knock sounded on the door; she could hear two men trying to argue in a whisper—John and Eric. She smiled and listened to them until she realized they had her red Fed-Ex box!

She jumped up and ran to open the door, grabbed the box, and slammed it shut before the two could even turn their heads. They merely stood and stared in stupefaction.

Her clothes! Thank God they'd made it there. She didn't care who had rerouted the clothes to the hotel, and she wasn't going to question Providence.

She spent only thirty seconds getting changed. She had no makeup, so she opened the door and stepped into the hallway.

John and Eric had made it three doors down when they heard her door open. They turned and their expressions at seeing Bethany Anne in her fashionable clothes and high heels, smiling at them, were priceless. Feeling like a woman again and not a vicious killing monster, she twirled around and asked, "You like?"

Neither one knew how to answer. John finally found his voice as he realized their hesitation did not please her at all. "Wow! I have no words to describe what I see, and 'like' is completely inappropriate!" He followed it up with what he hoped was the most handsome smile he owned.

Eric simply grinned, relieved his team leader had saved them both. She could take it any way she wanted, and they couldn't get in trouble with HR.

"John, you're making me happy I saved your ass. Let's go to lunch on me, I'm starving. Get whoever wants to go and we'll find a place."

Eric shook his head. "No can do. Some of us are stuck here filling in reports. If the brass hear about us taking time to go eat somewhere far away—and there are no good steak places near here—it will be our asses."

"You guys hold on." She walked back into her room and called to them to join her. Eric looked at his companion, who shrugged. "As far as I'm concerned, I wouldn't be here, so if she wants me to join her in her room, then I'll have to man up." He grinned at Eric as he walked toward her room. He could hear her plainly. "Miami is closer, but it'll still hurt like hell, Mr. Grimes."

"My bad, sorry, just wanted to make sure."

Bethany Anne pecked rapidly at her phone when they joined her in the room, and Eric shut the door.

She stopped and looked up. "How is everyone with hot dogs and hamburgers made fresh?"

## CHAPTER 14

**Florida City, FL, USA**

Almost the whole team was in the back parking lot. Half were already eating hot dogs, hamburgers, and Philly cheesesteak sandwiches and munching down on chili cheese fries, and a couple had ordered gator balls.

Bethany Anne sat under a tree nearby, enjoying her third Bronx Bomber sans onions.

Scott spoke to Eric as they waited in line.

"Hey, tell me the truth. Were you there when she ordered the food?"

"Yes, why?"

The queue moved forward a little.

"They say she just told the man in a scary voice to show up and start feeding us."

Eric laughed. "Scott, you should know her better. She didn't do any scary voice. She negotiated with them, and they agreed. I have nothing else to say. I told you I wouldn't talk about her behind her back. Not even about this, buddy."

They reached the front of the line, and a man looked out of the red food truck. It was actually a red trailer with a black-and-white checkered line running from the bottom to the top of the trailer. The serving window was the width of the two wheels in the back.

"Hey, buddy." The guy in the trailer caught their attention. "I can tell you. We have a place over on South Dixie. Been there a few years. I get a phone call that asks me to come over with the trailer, and I tried to explain we don't move from our spot. She asked if I would do it for some of America's finest and I said we could schedule it. She then asked me if she could schedule it in an hour for $25,000 before food costs and I told her I needed to get my trailer fixed, so maybe I could stop by on the way and here I am. So, you want a dog, a burger, or a sandwich?"

Scott didn't answer quickly enough as he was processing the story, so Eric ordered a Double Stack Chili Cheeseburger and gator balls. He looked at Scott. "You snooze, you lose, ya poser."

Bethany Anne sighed contentedly. She was finally full again, and all the guys seemed to be recovering. They were all professionals, but facing your mortality pulled the rug out from under your feet a little. Her phone beeped, and she pulled it out. Shit, she'd had it on voicemail and had missed a couple of calls.

The first was Ivan. He was with Stephen, and things were going well. He provided her with the vampire's new number and asked that she give him a call when she could.

The second was a voice message from Ecaterina. She wanted Bethany Anne to call Nathan or Gerry and talk to them about some Were issues. Not a problem.

First, she checked the time in Romania. About seven-ish at night...okay. She dialed Ivan. "Bethany Anne! Good to hear your voice. I take it things are fine in the States?"

"Good here at the moment, Ivan. Belly full of food and a good pair of shoes. What's up?"

"Nothing special. Stephen is a fast learner. I was concerned when you told me he knew nothing at all. Most times, not knowing something similar makes it harder for a person to catch on quickly."

"Treat him well, Ivan. He's a good guy, and I think he might be very important to me in the future. Also, stay close to him. I don't want you outside without his protection while you're there. I don't *know* anyone is watching, but I don't want to take any chances with you. I don't need to be the one to tell Ecaterina I got her favorite brother killed."

"No worries."

"Good. Where is Stephen?"

"One second." She could hear him walk through the house. "Stephen?"

"Yes?"

"Shit! Stephen, you have to stop sneaking up on me." She could almost imagine the vampire jumping out of the shadows to have fun at Ivan's expense.

"But, Ivan, it is the most fun I've had in ten years."

"That's because you've been asleep for ten years. Oh. Bethany Anne is on the phone."

"Why didn't you say that first?" Bethany Anne could hear them passing the phone. "Hello? My Queen?"

"Hello, Stephen, how are you doing?"

"I am beyond enjoying myself again. I am learning this new technology, and with the bagged blood, I'm dropping years each day. It is amazing."

"Stephen, will I have a little baby boy when I get back to Europe?"

He laughed. "No, Bethany Anne. I have never regenerated younger than when I was turned."

"When was that?"

"Twenty-five."

Bethany Anne tried to imagine what he would look like in his twenties and came up with nothing.

## QUEEN BITCH

"I'm sure you're a handsome rogue, Stephen. But no biting on the first date, understand?"

"My Queen, how could you think of me like that?" Stephen chuckled on the other end of the line.

"Because I know guys, you cad. Now, I need you to tell me straight. Are you up to contacting and working with the Pack Council there in Europe for me? I'm not talking about where they call you and kiss the vampire ground you walk on, but actually roll up your sleeves and work with them as equals? Okay, let's not go too far right now—mostly equals?" She smiled when she said the last part.

"Of course, my Queen. You have but to tell me what to do and I will make it happen."

"Great! I was hoping you still felt that way. Do you have a way to contact them or do I need to get you the info?"

"I'm sure I have a way to do this. There is a pack near here. You don't need to get your hands dirty. I will take care of it."

*Okay*, Bethany Anne thought. She loved a good subordinate who wasn't a cranky bitch. She was glad she never had herself as a subordinate. Maybe she owed her old boss Martin a thousand apologies. "Thanks, Stephen. Hey, did you get the room ready?"

"Of course. I did it the first night. Why, are you ready to use it?"

"No, not yet. I'm working on it."

**'*You're* working on it?**

***Stop interrupting, I'm talking here.***

**More like you're *lying* here. But go on.**

"Well, it is ready for you anytime."

"Great! Keep Ivan safe, okay?"

"I'll do that, and Bethany Anne, thank you."

"For what?"

"For calling and talking to me. It confirms what I knew that first night. You care about your relationships. I'll not fail you."

"I know, Stephen. Keep learning and touch base with the

Council. Make sure they aren't suffering from wanting to change the rules too much right now. Bye!"

"*La revedere.*"

She hung up, amazed the whole Stephen situation was going so well and Europe seemed like it might be in hand. She certainly hoped so because America seemed to be under attack.

She waved at Eric and Scott talking over by Joe's Famous Hot Dogs trailer. Everyone seemed to be in high spirits. Good.

John and Darryl looked at her. John gave her the universal "everything okay?" tilt of the head, and she smiled. She realized she hadn't had many people come by. There was at least a ten-foot clearing around her. No problem. She didn't think they would run away if she got up. She hoped they were merely giving her some personal space.

She went to the message from Ecaterina and listened to it one more time. First up, she decided to call Nathan. She hit his name on her phone and waited.

"Hey, what's up?"

"Thanks for calling, Bethany Anne. You got Ecaterina's message?"

"Yes. She said you guys have problems and need my input."

"More like serious issues and we are trying to figure out how to solve the problem without it becoming a bloodbath."

"Considering you're asking me, should I wonder if I'll want to create the bath?"

Nathan sighed. "That's about it in one. Where are you? Did you finish with Stephen yet and did you leave him in peace or pieces?"

She laughed. "You won't believe the story, which I will tell you later, but he has turned out to be a great guy. I'm here in Florida at the moment, hanging with Frank's team. We had an op last night, so I crashed at their hotel. I should be good to come up there if you need me."

"No, we can wait a few days. In fact, that might be best. Let me talk to Gerry again and plan this carefully. I would prefer we ambush all the troublemakers and let them make fools of themselves, but we would probably cause another Valentine's Day massacre. Weres tend not to make good decisions when confronted. We're kinda a hot-headed lot."

Sarcastically, Bethany Anne retorted, "I hadn't noticed during our altercation in Brasov, Nathan."

"Yeah, okay. You have a point. Let Gerry and me think about how to make it happen, and we'll get back to you when we have a couple of ideas. I really appreciate you working with us, Bethany Anne."

"No problem, Nathan. Take care of my girl, okay? I'll be up there in a day or two."

"Please, take a vacation. I'm sure you're tired after all your efforts. Why don't you relax for an extra month or so?"

She smiled. "If I was going to do that, I'd simply get a ticket for Ecaterina to come down here this evening."

Nathan backtracked quickly. "My mistake. See you in a couple of days."

"Yeah. Say hi to Ecaterina for me. Bye."

"Bye."

Bethany Anne hung up. Now that she had everything taken care of, she tried to think of what to do for a couple of days. Nathan must be doing well with Ecaterina to suggest she not come right away.

She needed to get to know the team better, and she was there, right after a good op. It would be stupid to leave right away.

Carefully, she considered what she could do to bring them together. Maybe a party at a bowling alley? No, too pretentious for these guys.

Bethany Anne laughed. There she was, all dressed up, and was now saying a bowling alley was too pretentious? She needed to get dressed in something a little more casual, and she did need transportation. Considering her options to find clothes, she pulled her phone out to look at what was available in the area.

On the other side of the trailer, Jesse Bivoreux had put his trash away and grabbed his Coke from the table with Joe's signage on it. He walked over to John and Darryl. "Hey, guys, congrats on getting those two Nosferatu last night. That was some scary shit." Bivoreux had been in the command ops van. He'd never been more scared in his life, and he had been pretty sure he was a dead man.

The trailer had shaken horribly while they suffered the constant banging by the Nosferatu trying to bust into the van. The men had drawn their sidearms and looked around by the light of the computer screens. Everyone's hearts were in overdrive. There had been some additional pistol shots outside, and he'd heard one of the Nosferatu fall off the roof. Then the banging had simply stopped. It grew quiet, and they'd heard the keening fade away as the Nosferatu all left the area. Two more quick sets of pistol shots had sounded and then, nothing.

Everyone had quickly picked the computer screens up. One of them had been unplugged. While it was rebooting, they had been able to watch the FLIR camera input and see that six Nosferatu were leaving the area, quickly chasing a single figure. According to the computer, they'd traveled at close to forty-five mph.

What happened next was totally unexplainable. The first figure stopped and waited for the six Nosferatu to catch up. When they did, the first contact simply disappeared. The FLIR operator looked beyond where the Nosferatu were, but there was nothing until the single figure appeared on screen again, moving from the same direction as before.

The next couple of seconds were almost too much to understand, even on replay. But it was obvious that the one who had come back in had kicked the asses of the Nosferatu and left none of them standing. Then it moved so fast back toward the command ops that the FLIR couldn't track it. Later, he would learn it had been the new vampire the team was working with, and he was incredibly impressed.

John and Darryl high-fived. "Got two, bieeeetch!" They laughed the laugh of the living. They knew how close it really had been.

"Say, tell me who that hot lady over there is?"

John and Darryl both looked around. "Where?" Puzzlement reflected on their faces.

He thought they were pulling his leg. "Right there on the ground, on her cell phone, you two ass-wipes. Why isn't anyone trying to talk her up?"

Their eyes grew really big as they followed his gaze and realized he was talking about Bethany Anne. They both realized that when they didn't look at her with the knowledge of the previous night's events, she had to be one of the most beautiful women in the world. Then their desire for self-preservation returned and the aspiration to pull a quick joke on Jesse quickly faded.

John could tell Darryl had voted him the spokesperson. Ass. "Jesse. That woman is our team leader."

Jesse looked at him. "John, you're shitting me again. Even I know you're the lead."

John tried again. How could he explain so Jesse understood without being crass? He respected Bethany Anne too much for that. "Jesse, I'm the team lead for the four of us. I take my lead from her, we got her back—do you understand?" He stared at Jesse, leaving him no room to misunderstand.

The truth dawned—she was the vampire. Blood drained from Jesse's face as he realized what he had said about her earlier. She was the one who had killed six Nosferatu in only a few seconds. He needed to go back to his room, so no one saw him with the shakes.

"Thanks. Congrats again, guys. I appreciate the heads-up. I'm going to go finish my reports." He threw his Coke in the trash can and didn't notice it bounced back out as he walked quickly back into the hotel.

John shook his head, picked up the empty, and dropped it in the trash. He did notice no one was talking with Bethany Anne. He suddenly wondered if she got lonely. Only one way to find out.

He walked over to her, and she looked up from her phone. "How are you doing?" She smiled up at him.

"I'm doing well, how do you feel? Having any desire for your steaks to be rare?"

That was like her, he thought. She wasn't afraid to get to the point. He sat down a few feet away. "No. Trusting you was the best decision I ever made. Honestly, it's done me a whole lot of good."

"How's that?" Bethany Anne was curious. She knew what might happen but wasn't sure.

"I had a long scar from a bad op a couple of years ago. It's gone. Tightness in my back right calf? Gone. No scar from last night at all. Can you tell me what happened?" He had wanted to ask her. In fact, half the time while talking to Darryl, he'd been psyching himself to ask. "Did I really call you a rectal hole dishrag?"

She laughed. "No, you dillweed. You called me a 'little rectal hole dictator.' You got ten points for that one!"

He smiled. He couldn't remember why he'd felt so uncomfortable with the thought of coming over earlier. He heard Darryl, Scott, and Eric come up behind him. Those fearless followers made sure he wasn't killed first. What a great backup team he had.

John's phone rang, and he looked at the caller ID. It was Dan Bosse. He answered. "What's up, boss?"

"John, we have a possible problem over in Miami. They have two SWAT situations, and their team is already engaged on op number one that's too far away. Apparently, it was a ruse, and the main hit is on a bank in the financial district. They're claiming they're terrorists, but we're pretty sure they're hiding a financial hit. We've been asked to see what we can do. We don't have to, and it feels almost mundane after all the shit we've been through. Do you and your team think you can help in any way?"

John looked at Bethany Anne and remembered she could hear anything around her. He raised an eyebrow. She knew he now considered her the real team leader. She reached down and took off her high heels. "I'll need a change of clothes."

Dan asked, "Did I just hear Bethany Anne?"

John agreed, "That you did, Dan."

"I hadn't meant to ask her. This isn't a Nosferatu takedown. I'm not objecting, just surprised."

"Yeah, well, imagine what the little shits will do when they find out Team Queen Bitch is on the way?" He smiled at Bethany Anne, who shook her head and then looked at each of them. She smiled and let her eyes go red.

Darryl whooped loudly, getting everyone's attention. "Look out, Miami. Queen Bitch is on the way!"

The guys all laughed and stood quickly. John stayed on the phone but whistled up everyone eating outside. Waving his hands in a circle, he walked on with Eric at his side. Scott helped Bethany Anne to her feet, and he and Darryl fell in behind her.

Those who had seen them leave the helicopter recognized the team had stepped back into ops mode. Guys all around shoved their food into their mouths and dropped plates off and sodas in the can. As one, they rushed inside for a briefing on the next op.

Yup, they were going back into action and would kick some ass.

Guaran-fucking-teed.

## CHAPTER 15

**Miami, FL, USA**

Dan tried to pull the information together while the van raced through the traffic. It wasn't the smoothest of rides, and the vehicle had some issues left over from last night. He pulled the best information he could from the Miami PD. TQB, as they had become known in the last hour, was out shopping. They only had a little of what she needed—the vest and a shirt she could use, but no pants.

The guys had stopped at a leather shop, and Bethany Anne had actually agreed to wear some black leather pants. Dan had to shake his head. He would never have imagined a day when he worked for a vampire and liked it. But he couldn't help himself. That woman was a complete badass, but she didn't always take herself too seriously. She was the perfect complement of respect and laughter, and the cuss words she and her team came up with were hilarious.

The guys at the ops center begged them to wear mics and cameras. While Carl and Bill had used them frequently, Bethany Anne was absolutely against cameras. She didn't mind them audio-recording the op, though. Dan had looked at John to see if he could get some support for visuals, but he'd merely shaken his head in the negative.

They said to never give a command you knew would be ignored, so he hadn't even requested the team to wear the video cameras. Maybe he could get building security footage later?

Bethany Anne traveled with the guys in the SUV they'd originally used to pick her up. She sat between Scott and Darryl. John and Eric took the front again, with Eric driving. She really felt good. Her team was gelling, and she began to think of it as truly *her* team.

She found the team name a little less than thrilling, but what did she want? Team 'We kick your ass and slap your father?' She could be bitchy at times. Besides, it beat Team 'Murder & Mayhem,' which was honestly truth-in-advertising. It would come out later, at any rate, and it might as well put the focus on her.

For those who wanted to see her in an ugly light, the name would galvanize them around it. For those who wanted to believe she was a good girl, it hopefully caused them to pause a minute. Either way, it had already stuck, and nothing short of her having a raging bitch attack would change it. So, Queen Bitch it was, for better or worse.

*Ah, fuck it. Time to live up to the hype.*

"John, what's the word from Dan?"

"Not too much and none of it good. They hit the Southeast Financial Center right after lunch. Their early morning heist in Pompano Beach was real. They got the SWAT stuck in good there before they struck downtown. Now, all they have are regular cops. The National Guard might be able to help, and the FBI will probably be there as well. This could be a real political dick-beating we have to deal with, Bethany Anne. It won't make you any friends if it gets out you aren't a team player."

"What do you mean? I've got you guys with me."

"What smooth operator over here is trying to say…" Darryl

explained, "is that you will have bias against us if they find out you're not playing on Team Human."

The car went quiet at that pronouncement. Bethany Anne considered how she felt about being something other than human, considering she got to live a longer life. Probably hundreds or maybe thousands of years longer. Now her ability to help people was off the charts, she decided they would have to get over themselves. But it did raise the reality that she would need protection and a good place to rest.

"Aw, fuck 'em if they can't take a joke, right, guys?" She winked into the mirror so Eric could see it.

"Hell, yeah!" Eric hit the steering wheel. "They say to make your weakness your strength, right? Why don't we make up fang badges with Queen Bitch on the logo and we can act like complete badasses with pretend fangs and red contacts?"

The rest loved the idea. Bethany Anne merely put her face in her hands. Gods, what would she do with this team? On the one hand, she hated it. On the other, it was fantastic. Shit, she could have a pair of fake fangs and red contacts that actually could be used. "Eric, I hate it, but it's genius. Can we get anything like that before we hit the bank?"

Darryl and Scott both pulled out their smartphones while John called back to Agent Bosse to let him know they had to make another slight detour and a short stop on the way to the building.

Scott found it first, only about eight blocks out of their way. They stopped right in front of the store, blocking the road. John reached under his seat, flicked a portable cop light on, and stuck it to the roof of the SUV. Barely two minutes later, Scott jumped back in the van with two brown bags full of vampire teeth and three sets of red contact lenses. "We all need the teeth, not just Bethany Anne. They only had three sets of the contacts, but I figure we can order from Amazon and get them tomorrow wherever we need them."

Bethany Anne struggled with her emotions. Until the team had welcomed her, she hadn't realized how alone she had felt. Stephen was the first step toward acceptance, but these guys were human, and they didn't shrink away and fear her.

She had heard Agent Bivoreux talk earlier in the day. She'd resented the coarse discussion of her looks a little, but she also couldn't fault him too much. She knew she was still changing, and she suspected TOM had something to do with it. Her bra size had gone up a cup already. So, either she was too good-looking, or all the guys knew she was a vampire and it completely sucked the life out of their acceptance.

She had known she wouldn't be part of society when she took the job, but she hadn't realized what a change simply existing could make. Hell, even the animals back when she was on the mountain in Romania were freaked out by her.

These guys were keepers.

---

The team pulled into the cordoned-off area after John showed his badge. They spilled from the vehicle and walked over to the ops command van, and John knocked on the door. A second later, Agent Bosse opened it and stepped out. There was no way the five of them would fit inside.

Dan smiled. He wasn't sure what would happen, but he knew it would be good. "This is what I have. There are probably three different groups in the building. One group has the hostages. One is hacking in the server room, and one is in the basement doing God only knows what. We intend to save the hostages first and then go after the other two."

Bethany Anne chimed in, "Do you know who the main hack is against?"

"Not at this time. There are three of the biggest fifty financial companies in this building. It could be any of them or all of them."

"Wait one second." She pulled her phone out and called Nathan again. A couple of rings later, he answered. "Nathan, Bethany Anne. Hey, are you protecting any of these three companies?" She named them. "Yeah, we're on an op, and it looks like the hit might be against one or all of them. There's a group in the server room right now. Yes, okay. Thanks." She hung up.

"I have a friend who works with financial firms. He's in the electronic and digital security profession. He says all three are clients and have been targeted by some pretty effective penetration tactics in the last two months. He wouldn't be surprised if they're hitting them internally because the digital attack wasn't successful.

"Also seems like they're pressed for time," John said.

Eric didn't follow that. "Pressed for time?"

Bethany Anne completed the thought. "Yeah, if their hackers have been at it for eight weeks, and these two ops would take a couple of weeks at least to plan..."

Dan interrupted. "I'd say four if you include the necessary casing of the buildings at two locations. So, they worked for one month on electronic means and then took four weeks to get ready for this. They could have tried half a year or more on the digital side before getting lucky. I see your point, John."

He nodded.

"All right. We think the hostage situation is legitimate. They'll give up two per hour for the next few hours and then they'll either disappear or blow the building and escape. I'm concerned the group in the basement is locating the main structural pillars that hold up the building. Blow them, and the whole thing collapses—or enough of it to matter. How they get out is another question. I've requested underground plans to see if they might plan to leave through an old shaft or something."

Bethany Anne looked at him. Dan raised his hands. "Just making sure! Maybe I've seen too many Hollywood movies."

"Hey, whatever happened to the blood from last night?" she asked him.

"Should still be around. Why, will you need some?"

"Maybe. John, can you get us about four packs?"

John looked at her. "Do you need a particular type?"

"Yeah, give me an unpretentious B negative. No, you ass. Whatever he thinks he can do without will work fine."

John nodded to Darryl who left to find the blood.

Dan spoke again. "So, how will you get into the building without attracting notice? We know all obvious entrances and a few others have been booby-trapped. We can tell that a lot of encrypted video transfers are happening. We think that means they've planted video cameras to watch us out here as well."

Bethany Anne turned one way and then the other, looking at the buildings beside them. The Southeast Financial Center was a very nice fifty-five story office building with a stepped top and a fifteen-story parking garage next door. It was higher than the multiple buildings around it. Damn, she wanted the roof. "Any chance we can get a helicopter for my team and me? Also, a crew that won't see or speak about anything that happens?"

Dan considered that for a moment, then turned and opened the door to the van. A second later, a phone was handed to him. "Frank? It's Dan. Yeah, we made it over here just fine. Bethany Anne has a plan… No, no, I don't know the plan, and neither, I suspect, will you. She wants a helicopter with a deaf and mute crew. Yup, completely silent and never knew anything. How long? That long? Hold on, she wants the phone."

Bethany Anne took it from him. "What's the problem? Is it the helicopter or can you not promise they won't talk? Ah, so a senior officer could order them to talk? Well, I can take care of the not talking part. No. No, it wouldn't be by killing them. Look, you have your secrets, let a woman have hers, okay? Still that long? Shit! Okay. Work your magic, and I'll try to work mine."

She handed the phone back to Dan, retrieved her cell phone, and started researching local helicopter charter companies. When she found a likely solution, she entered the phone number.

This really had to work out.

## CHAPTER 16

**Miami, FL, USA**

Captain William 'Bobcat' Carlson tinkered on his love, a 2002 UH-60L Black Hawk helicopter. The Army had upgraded to the UH-60M and Bobcat had been able to get one of the retired units. Usually, he flew a Hiller UH-12C for most of his commissions, but his love was for the Black Hawk. If it hadn't been such an expensive beast to fly, he would do it all the time.

He had just finished up and closed up the engine compartment door when his phone rang.

"Bobcat Aviation, this is Bill speaking. Where can we fly you today?"

He heard a pleasant female voice ask him about his availability for flying immediately. "Yes, I'm open today. Will it be you and another, or just you?" Hey, she sounded good on the phone—maybe it would be a long flight. Since leaving the military a couple of years back, he was doing okay, but the business took all his time. His opportunities to meet women were seriously curtailed. Besides, the Black Hawk already demanded all his money. There wouldn't be any left to share with another woman. The Black Hawk was a jealous girlfriend.

"You're asking about the Black Hawk? Yes, it's available as well, but it would be really expensive, ma'am. About $5,000 an hour. How much for the rest of the day?" Crap, this was fantastic—getting to fly the Black Hawk and actually make money instead of sucking gas fumes. *Thank God.*

"I can cut you a deal at $35,000, but that isn't total air time. That simply means you have my attention for the rest of the day until midnight. Any extra fuel over five hundred miles will be added to the bill."

Bill grew concerned. "You need me downtown? I can't. The aviation rules won't permit me to do that. Yes, if you take care of the red tape, I can get out there. Ma'am, if I start now before I get approval, you will get a bill for $5,000. That's a big risk. Okay, I'll do it."

Bill took the credit card info and went to his computer. She had told him to put a hold on the credit card for $50,000 and damned if it didn't go through.

He whistled as he hurried over to the little electric four-wheeler he used to push the helicopter out of the hangar. He was going for a ride, whether he got the job or not. $5,000 would be enough for the gas and at least an hour of playing, and he would still have enough for the rent this month.

Ten minutes later, he received an incoming call from Washington DC that gave him clearance and the coordinates of his pickup. Son of a bitch. He was also told this was for a police action, and that according to his military jacket, he had the security clearance to know how to keep his mouth shut. While he couldn't be ordered, it would be appreciated. The veiled threat was that if he opened his mouth, life could become hard.

Although it rankled that someone would try to put the screws to him, he never talked about any of his clients. He certainly wouldn't talk about a woman who had a credit card that didn't even flinch at a $50k approval.

He went through the preflight, obtained his clearance, and took the bird aloft, heading downtown.

He landed in a large park in the middle of a soccer field with three large black SUVs parked on one side. Men walked the perimeter, making sure no one came close to his landing spot. As he set down, the second SUV pulled out onto the field. It stopped a few feet outside the main rotor wash, the door opened, and four guys in black fatigues with full battle rattle emerged. And, holy hotdogs in heaven, a female in battle rattle but with black leather pants joined them. If she had been the lady on the phone, he certainly wouldn't talk to anyone about her. Damn, he wished it was a flight for one.

One man opened the door, and he and his buddy stepped in. The lady boarded third, and the final two heaved themselves in and closed the door. The lady came forward. "Mr. Carlson?"

Bill picked up a second pair of headphones and handed them back. Bethany Anne put them on and immediately, it helped compensate for the loudness of the helicopter. "That's so much better. So, let's try this again. Mr. Carlson?"

"Yes, but call me Bill or Bobcat. It's my nickname."

"From the service?"

"Yes."

"All right, Bobcat. My name is Bethany Anne and behind you is my team leader John, plus Eric, Darryl, and Scott. I need you to take us to within a hundred feet above the Southeast Financial Center. Hover there for sixty seconds after I pat you on the shoulder and then leave, heading in the same direction for five miles. After that, I want you to simply fly wherever you want to. I have your cell phone number, so if I need you, I'll call you. Make sense?"

"Yes. Fly over to Southeast Financial Center. Count to sixty after the tap, fly straight five miles, and then pretty much wherever I want. You'll call if you need me."

"Right, but make sure you have enough fuel if I need you, okay?"

He grinned. It would mean he'd touch down a couple of extra times, but that was fine. "Sure, no problem. I'll fly into a nearby airport for fuel in case you call me while I'm on the ground."

"Sounds good. Let's go."

She handed the headphones back. Damn, he wouldn't be able to get her number. Wait, he had it on his cell phone already. Sweet!

The Black Hawk helicopter landing in the park was the main topic for the local kids for a week. Finally, a school fight became the new topic when a teacher got punched in the nose.

As they approached the tower, she turned to her team. "All right, if you aren't comfortable with trusting me, now's the time to admit it and pussy out. Anybody in the 'not trusting' category, raise your hand."

All of them merely smiled at her; she smiled back. "Okay, we're about to do something that is team-only. I don't want this getting out, because it can and will be used against you and me. I'll get each of you down to the top of the building from the helicopter. Darryl, you and Scott will go second. Make sure you have those blood bags. Let me have one now."

Bethany Anne took a bag and drank, a little self-conscious doing it around the guys. John winked at her.

When the Black Hawk slowed they double-checked their gear, and Bethany Anne moved both Scott and Darryl back and told them, "On pain of death, you two wank-lickers better not move an inch, you understand?" They each grabbed a handhold and promised themselves nothing could make them move from the spot. She nodded to Eric, who opened the door, then looked out quickly and down at the top of the building below. She leaned over to the pilot and patted him on the shoulder, then turned and ran toward the door, grabbed John and Eric in a vice-like grip, and they disappeared.

Scott and Darryl were shocked. They wanted to look to see if they were splattered over the rooftop or not. The next thing they knew, she was back in the helicopter, closed the door, and grabbed them. Fifteen seconds later, the chopper left the airspace and headed toward Hollywood, Florida. Bobcat was the only one in the aircraft.

Down below, the team shook off their surprise, put their op faces on, and started toward the door into the building. They found the main stairway and headed down. Floor numbers were painted on the doors in green, making it easy to keep track of their location.

Bethany Anne left them at level forty-seven. By the time she returned, they had made it to twelve and were breathing hard. Down was better than up, but it still wasn't easy.

She advised them that the group in the basement had been wiring up explosives to take the building down. A newly made hole led to a tunnel, and their team would exit there if possible.

While she filled them in, she let them rest. The terrorists were in contact with each other every three minutes. That meant they had three minutes to take care of everything.

The narrow window sucked.

She asked for any ideas. Eric suggested they split up. She could take a group, and two teams of two could go after the other two groups.

The plan worked for her. The first priority was the safety of the hostages. Then the charges in the basement. She wanted the last pair to focus on the computers since she wanted the intruders to answer a few questions. She took the second bag of blood from Darryl and drank the contents. Moving them down from the Black Hawk hadn't taxed her energy too much, but she hadn't topped up, either. She didn't really want to drink the coppery tasting stuff, so she only did it in a situation that required extraordinary actions. Two bags left. She told Darryl to give one to Eric so both teams would have one if she needed it.

Scott gave them each a set of fake fangs, they played a quick game of rock, paper, scissors, and Eric was the first loser. The other three put in their contact lenses, which didn't create too much of a hindrance to their eyesight. On an op with a huge chance to blow up into a PR nightmare, they needed to make sure Bethany Anne's heritage, as recent as it was, was hidden in broad daylight.

So to speak.

They all, including Bethany Anne, put their fangs in a pocket of their vest. No one could talk well while wearing them, but they would use them later after the main hit if they needed to.

There were smiles all around. The men were vets, hardened in battle against the Nosferatu. Their reaction times had been honed against pros even SpecOps teams couldn't compete with. The team had taken down two on their own and had come out of the meat grinder whole on the other side. Now, they had the best fucking leader in the world who trusted them to get the job done. They wouldn't fail her or the hostages downstairs.

It was time to party.

They made their way carefully to the fifth floor and the server rooms. Scott and Darryl stepped out of the stairwell, signaled back toward the door that they were clear, and headed slowly to the area where the intruders were hacking the computers.

Bethany Anne stopped at the main floor and motioned John and Eric to signal her when in place.

The minute it took them to get ready allowed her to focus her hearing on what was up with the situation with the hostages. She heard a few women and one man crying. A couple of times, she heard someone struck by the stock of a gun and a huge number of threats. Bethany Anne grew pissed. Her eyes glowed red, and her fangs had grown involuntarily to the longest length they ever had. No one would mistake her fangs for fakes right then.

She fucking hated it when someone in a position of power took advantage of others. She wondered what these assholes would do if the tables were turned? Would they shout and berate others if they were helpless? She heard one woman scream to her child to come back to her. That decided it—she was going in early. As she opened the door, she heard the click.

*Good timing, men. Good timing.* She clicked a reply and hurtled into the first man without even slowing down. He had his rifle poised to strike a toddler who was crying and running blindly. She backhanded the man, throwing his body, now headless, back into a large decorative tree in the lobby. The corpse hit the trunk and stopped, then slumped over.

The two insurgents closest to her had waited to see the expected attack on the child. Their faceplates each received two .45 rounds, blowing chunks of their helmets out the backs of their heads and peppering the hostages on the floor with brain matter and plastic. That, unfortunately, couldn't be helped.

The last three men were on the opposite side of the room, and she couldn't run through the crowd. Fortunately, the room had thirty-foot-high ceilings. She raced to a wall and kicked backward off it, aimed her jump over the hostages, and then used her ability to slip through the Etheric to appear twenty feet in the air right above the middle tango. She fired the first shot as gravity took over, and all three were dead before she'd dropped ten feet. She landed by the first man, who now sprawled on the ground with blood draining from the holes in the top of his head. Swiftly, she ducked behind a decorative tree and slipped back through the Etheric to the safety of the stairwell. There, she clicked her comm once to confirm her task was complete.

She raced up the stairs, back to level five. The group in the basement had three members, but she was confident her men could take them out.

Down below, John and Eric had eased into the room and blocked the stairway door from closing, so it didn't make a sound. They weren't sure how Bethany Anne had made it in and out but wouldn't break radio silence to ask.

John felt alive, even more alert than the previous night if that were possible. It seemed everything was crystal clear, and he was definitely in the zone. He pointed at Eric and then pointed at the guy near the exit.

Their team had only one rule of engagement. The enemy needed to be terminated. That was the rule. The corollaries all had to do with, 'If this type of supernatural, use silver frangibles. If this other type, use the prescribed ammunition.' For humans, lead worked well. Maybe if someone had thought about it, they might have activated different rules, but no one seemed to remember to do that. Oh, well, tough shit for the infiltrators.

Eric was quiet as he prepared to attack his target. He gave John the "ready in five" sign and started the countdown. On the final count, he stood and dropped the terrorist, who had been looking into the newly made four-foot hole in a back wall. They had pulled out some old computer racks on wheels and apparently used them as a protective wall and set off a demo. The floor was a mess. Now his tango had two bullet holes in the back of his head, and his blood was all over the wall.

Eric heard one set of shots behind him, and he turned quickly. There should have been two. He hurried around the corner and found the first dead terrorist. Looking up, he saw John walk over to the second dead man. Somehow, he had blasted both targets and fired fast enough that it sounded like one shot. *Son of a bitch, that's incredible.*

They heard Bethany Anne's click of success and responded with their own. With no time to waste, they examined the explosives and realized they weren't set up for remote detonation. Thankfully, the wires all went to a master control by the fresh tunnel exit. They had had some experience with disarming explosives, but without a really good reason, they wouldn't take any chances. Instead, they moved the box as far away from the exit as they could and prepped a defensive position, aiming into the tunnel. They had the responsibility to ensure nothing attacked the team from there. The rest of the group had to make sure their backs were covered, and since Bethany Anne was behind them, security was assured.

Up above, Darryl and Scott heard the second set of clicks. It was their turn.

They moved around the corner, and each put a silenced bullet into the lookout's legs. Scott took the right, and Darryl took the left. The man fell in pain and surprise and didn't see the two rush up beside him. Scott lifted the guard high enough that Darryl could grab the badge and slot it in place. At the same time, Scott grabbed the man's right hand and placed it over the security glass. Sensing both the live handprint and the badge, the door unlocked. Scott dropped him back to the ground. Darryl shot him in the head as the door opened.

"Let me go in first, guys." Darryl started a little, not expecting Bethany Anne right beside him. He quickly pulled his focus back to his task, but it was close.

Crouching, Darryl moved sideways, and Bethany Anne moved ahead so fast it seemed she was running in a crouch. He and Scott took up positions on the inside of the door, facing out. The vampire knew she had insurgents ahead; they were safe from that position.

The inside of the server room was loud. With so many rows of server racks, there were probably over a thousand machines in the space. Almost all ran fan systems that made it sound like little jets taking off every time they spun up to cool down the machines. The little 1U & 2U units could be really loud in enclosed spaces.

Three hackers stood separately in different places in the server room. All of them had rested their short bullpup rifles on the floor, leaning against the rack as they worked.

Bethany Anne recognized the design, though not the make. The weapon worked by moving the firearm's action and magazine behind the trigger to save weight and gain maneuverability, while not sacrificing accuracy from a shorter barrel.

The firearms didn't matter. None of the men heard when she knocked a hacker in the back of his head with her forearm. Unfortunately, she killed the first one because she didn't think about the difference between a Were's hard head and a human's.

Within seconds, she had two unconscious guys and one dead one. One of the living was a female—teach her to be gender biased. She signaled Scott to take the female and threw the male over her shoulder in a fireman's hold. Scott took the second in the same way, and they hurried down the stairs. She could hear the commotion from the hostages as they passed the main level. It sounded chaotic as people hurried out. Bethany Anne hoped it wouldn't become a stampede, but she couldn't show herself. She and her team needed to get the hell out of Dodge. She sure hoped the exit went somewhere or there would be egg on her face. She did *not* want to call on Frank to help get her team out. How embarrassing would that be?

They reached the basement and saw the three bodies and the defensive position Eric and John had set up. Darryl took over from Scott to give him a rest. Bethany Anne gave John the guy she carried, and he took the load without too much trouble. That enabled her to go into the tunnel unencumbered.

She was able to make good time and followed a significantly long stretch that took two doglegs until it hit a regular underground drainage pipe system that went both left and right. The doglegs were probably intended to reduce the blowback from the collapse of the building. Well, that wouldn't happen now.

No one waited for her when she poked her head out of the dogleg. The infiltrators must have thought they would have an advance team. Tough shit. Bethany Anne had the winning team, and to the victor went the spoils—namely, contestants number one and two whom they carried with them.

She grabbed her phone and turned on the mapping function. As she'd surmised, she was close enough to the surface to get a reading. They were under NE 2nd Avenue. Another hole was located forty-five feet down the tunnel to her right. She moved forward and into the hole. It stopped after only a few feet at a metal ladder leading upward, which she climbed. Reaching the top, she pushed aside a heavy grate and entered a metal building. She could see that they had hidden their efforts by making it look like the structure was under renovation. No one was there, but a quick look revealed two windowless white vans parked outside with "John's Building Contractors" and a cell phone number painted on the sides in poor handwriting. Both looked pretty rundown. That was obviously how they got in and out of the building without raising suspicion.

Satisfied, she turned back down the passages and met the team as they exited into the drainage sewers. She explained the plan, and the bodies were transferred one more time. She took the guy from John, and Eric took the girl from Darryl. The three without the hackers hurried up the ladders, ditched much of their weaponry, and found a couple of shirts with paint all over them. They checked the vans, and both had keys tucked under the front seats. Scott drove one away, parked it in a daily parking lot, and jogged back. John circled the block until they were ready.

On his fourth lap around the block, Scott signaled to him that it was time. They opened the metal security door, and John simply drove the van over the curb and halfway into the shop. The terrorists must have removed the front wall behind the security door for that purpose. The van doors were slid open and the hackers were placed inside while Eric loaded the gear into the back. John moved to the front passenger seat, and Eric took the wheel.

Scott stopped traffic by simply standing in the street. It wasn't like any cops nearby weren't already at the Southeast Financial Center. No one would race over here in the next minute.

Bethany Anne entered the van. There was no need for her face to be caught by security cameras on the street if there were any.

Darryl and Scott jumped in, and Eric pulled casually away, sticking his arm out the window in a friendly wave to the cars honking behind him.

Bethany Anne immediately called Bobcat. She had located a lot on Google Maps about eight miles away in South Miami. She wanted him to land there. He had been flying off the coast near Palmetto Bay, so it wasn't too far from him. He headed north toward the pickup zone.

Landing, he saw a beat-up white van with some building contractor's name and number on the side. It moved over the field toward him, so he hoped it was his people.

Considering the permissions to fly over downtown in a Black Hawk and the knowledgeable person who talked to him on the phone about his security clearance, he easily deduced he was working with a team helping with the terrorist operation. He didn't know how they had dropped from his helicopter, so he would never have to lie, anyway. All he did know was that they hadn't left any gear hooked up behind.

He simply assumed they had something new the military didn't want anyone to know about yet.

Sure enough, the doors opened, and he picked up not only his original team, but two newcomers that looked...yup, they were out of it. He saw no blood, so they were probably alive but unconscious. Two of the team had paint-spattered shirts over their gear. Bobcat wasn't sure what that was about, but he was sure someone had a good story. Not that he would ever hear it.

They emptied the van of their gear, loaded up the chopper, and Bethany Anne gave him the signal to take them up. She sat beside John. "Does Dan have a place he wants us to land?"

"No, nothing yet. All hell's breaking loose at the location. With all the hostages leaving so quickly, it took a minute for the cops to get past them and into the building. They found the dead from group one and the guys in the server room. Since we didn't change anything, they know two 'got away,' and Dan says they're providing updates about the situation in the basement. Everyone will clear the building until they confirm the demolition charges are neutralized. He can't leave just yet—too much pandemonium, and it would look strange for a support vehicle to try to leave."

She nodded, putting on the extra pair of headphones from the chopper. A tap on Bobcat's shoulder got his attention.

"How's it going?"

He glanced at Bethany Anne with a smile and quickly resumed watching his forward focus. "Really? You're asking me how it's going when I'm back in some action with my baby here?" He patted his girl with love. "Where do you want to go now?"

"Uh, somewhere a Black Hawk helicopter won't make the news?"

He laughed. "Lady, Black Hawks always make the news. Didn't you know that?"

She grimaced. Perhaps it wasn't the best choice for an unobtrusive getaway. How could she turn it around?

"Okay, let's do this. Take me sightseeing where the most expensive homes are. Your story is you had a very wealthy and eccentric lady hire your services who wanted this helicopter. I didn't care about the price, but I'm looking at homes."

Bobcat smiled. This was what he lived for. Hot dames, hot guns, and hot times. Hell yeah!

"You got it. We're close to the best of Coral Gables; we'll head down the beach. You want to be seen, right?"

"You got it, I'll flaunt it."

This would be the best PR he could ever receive. Bethany Anne maneuvered into the co-pilot's seat. She was pretty damn limber.

She searched for properties using her cell phone, found one she liked going for 8.9 million dollars, and called the broker. The woman answered, and she told her she wanted to see the house immediately. The agent said she would close out her late lunch and drive right over, and did Bethany Anne need directions?

"No, no directions. I'll just see where my pilot can land nearby." She hung up.

"Hey, Bobcat. Here's a house I want to see. It has a pool so if you can hover over it, I can wash some of this blood off my hands by jumping in. That would be pretty eccentric, don't you think?"

"I think it would be crazy, but then I like crazy. Or, you could use the baby wipes that are under your seat. I use them to get the oil off when I work on the engines."

Bethany Anne reached under the seat and pulled out a half-used tub of baby wipes. They did a bang-up job cleaning her hands, and she pulled a fresh one to clean her face. Now, she smelled like a baby's bottom.

The house she wanted to see was in Smugglers Cove in Key Biscayne, so Bobcat angled the Black Hawk over the water. The house was near the Bill Baggs Cape Florida State Park. He was able to find a decent landing spot that didn't upset the wealthy neighbors, and Bethany Anne jogged over to the house. She jumped a fence and slipped through the Etheric and across the canal when no one was looking. The area had no desire for unwanted visitors of either the animal or human variety.

She arrived at the house with the help of her phone just as the real estate agent pulled up.

The real estate lady arrived in a late model BMW 5 series. Her name was Nancy, and she was decked out in an expensive white suit and a beautiful pair of Brian Atwoods Bethany Anne had to admire. Comparing the woman's garb to her present outfit, she felt like she was slumming. Then again, she had the money to buy the house. So, fuck it.

"Are you Nancy?"

"Are you...Bethany Anne?" Nancy wasn't convinced this wasn't a prank. How the so-called client had got into the subdivision was beyond her.

"Yes, sorry about the look, but I was having a Rambo day when I spotted the house. I asked my pilot to land over there in the state park. I'll make this quick. I don't think they want the Black Hawk staying there too long."

"Um, Black Hawk? Isn't that a military helicopter?"

"Yup." Bethany Anne pointed to her outfit. "I had to dress appropriately. I just love your Brian Atwoods!" She used the most kissy-smoochy voice she could dredge up when talking about Nancy's shoes.

That cinched it. Any lady who played Rambo with a helicopter for the afternoon and could recognize her rather exclusive and expensive pair of Brian Atwoods was indisputably a good client for her.

It took about ten minutes for Bethany Anne to decide she wanted the house.

Nancy asked her what she wanted to counteroffer on the 8.9 million asking price, and Bethany Anne decided to play it to the hilt. "What do I care if I can get the house for one or two million less? Negotiating is a pain in the ass. When I want something, I buy it. Let me call my secretary to work with you to finalize the deal. She's a European who has just come over to America with me. So be a little patient with her, okay?"

Nancy assured her she would be the epitome of patience.

Bethany Anne retrieved her phone and called Ecaterina. "Hi, Ecaterina, listen, I'll give you the contact information for a real estate agent working a deal with me for a property outside Miami. Oh, Nathan is there? That's a complete shock. So yes, work with him on the particulars, but I'll purchase it for 8.9 million dollars. I'll send you her contact information and a link to the property as well as a check. Yes, I'll probably be back in two days now. Okay, bye."

She hung up and texted her Nancy's information. "Okay, got to go! You have my phone number, but I'd rather not deal with this while I'm playing. Ta ta!" With that, she left Nancy to close the house up.

Well, one base of operations was now accomplished. She

wasn't entirely sure why she wanted one there, but it seemed to be a focus for the Nosferatu so it might work out well.

She would have to get Ecaterina to move down there. Besides, ice was a bitch in high heels up north in the winter.

She jogged back, jumped the fence again, and slipped back through the Etheric to make it across the canal and to the helicopter, which was winding up the rotors again. Darryl, Scott, and Eric stood around and looked fierce, and when she jumped on board, she saw John with a pistol, watching her two hackers who were now awake and very, very scared.

The team climbed in and closed the door, and the pilot got out of there. Dan had called while Bethany Anne was busy. They had finally escaped the madhouse at the Financial Center and were going out to the airport where Bobcat's company was located. They planned to meet at the hangar when he landed.

That worked for her.

"I see my two contestants have woken up. Did they have anything to say?"

John shook his head. "Outside of who are we, where are we, and claiming all sorts of innocence? Nope."

She looked down at the two hackers. If it was true that they were innocent, she might be able to use them. She couldn't concentrate well enough with the helicopter racket to deal with them right then. Well, that wasn't true. She could have, but she didn't want to.

Bethany Anne nodded and slid back into the co-pilot's seat. She really liked this helicopter, she decided as she put the headset back on. "Heya, Bobcat, how they hanging?"

"One beside the other, sister, one beside the other." She smiled at his easy-going attitude. She really liked the chopper and the pilot.

"So, did you buy it?"

"The house?"

"Yup."

"Yeah, I liked it. I have a team member working on the details, but it should close in a couple of days at the most. Looks like I'll be in Miami more often now."

Bobcat was truly nonplussed. This lady had really bought a house in Smugglers Cove? The place was notorious for huge homes with price tags that could easily buy less expensive helicopters a couple of times over.

"Need a pilot on your team?" He smiled to take the seriousness out of the question, trying to make it sound like a joke.

"Actually, Bobcat, I think I need a pilot who has access to a Black Hawk who wouldn't mind becoming a member of my team. It includes purchasing his whole business, and upgrading his equipment with some items a few people might not...shall we say, appreciate? Know anyone who might be interested?"

He darted a look at her. She had stopped the fun-loving bimbo act and now showed him a very serious face.

He looked back out through the windshields. "Hell yeah, let's get this baby on the ground and talk."

"It could be dangerous."

"How often?"

She shrugged. "Beats the hell out of me. In the last month, I've been in four firefights, been shot once, had to kill or incapacitate over twenty-five people, torture one, and other stuff. John back there was stabbed—seriously—only last night. Still interested?"

He glanced back at her. If she didn't have four badass men in his helicopter and two obvious hostages and government connections, he would have questioned her statement. The way she explained it so matter-of-factly made it obvious she didn't think it was a big deal. He glanced at the back of the chopper one more time and had a gut check. If she was offering to let him join this kind of team, he wanted in.

"I've been dying on the vine, sister. Maintaining this baby is the only thing keeping me sane. I don't know why the hell I planted myself here in Miami. I mostly get to ferry around the people playing on the beach. This is the first truly interesting charter I've had in the last year. Anything else?"

"Yeah, but it'll have to wait until we get down, and the four in my team and you will have to get together and talk."

"Looking forward to it."

Bethany Anne looked out the chopper window and had her own conversation with TOM about his efforts for a usable serum until they landed. She wasn't sure of the outcome, but things were slowly coming together.

Bobcat landed the chopper outside his hangar at the airport. Three additional vehicles were parked alongside, including a white cargo van and another van with a quick patch on the door. Not exactly the most interesting or expensive vehicles around, but the hard cases he could see looked like his type of guys. Damn, it felt good to be involved in something real again. There was no drug like adrenaline to make one feel alive. The quickest way to get it was through danger. Maybe subconsciously, that was why he'd hung it all on the line and put everything into his Black Hawk. It wasn't fat cats who wanted this type of ride. It was the people who needed the real deal, and he wanted to be there with them.

Now, he had hooked an opportunity, and he couldn't reel it in fast enough. All he could do was ride it out into the sunset, however long that took him. It sounded like it could be as little as a few weeks. Well, fuck it. He only lived one life, so best it not be a boring one.

The team exited the helicopter quickly and professionally and took their two hostages over to the van and handed them off to someone inside. Another guy stepped out of the vehicle, and it looked to Bobcat like he was a leader of some sort. The pilot finished his landing checks and finally slid out himself.

He noticed Bethany Anne walking to the group by the van. Man, what a looker. Why the rest of the guys didn't glance surreptitiously at that ass, he had no idea, but he doubted he would stay on the payroll if he got caught doing it. He left the chopper and went to get his four-wheeler to move the Black Hawk inside the hangar.

Bethany Anne caught his attention. "Moving the chopper in?"

"Yeah. Need me to leave it?"

"Maybe. How long does it take to get it back out again?"

"Just a few minutes."

"Oh, Okay. Go ahead, and I'll join you after you're done."

Bethany Anne turned to Dan. "Hey, I need to ask you a few questions about how this outfit works. Can I have some of your time?"

"Now?"

"Yes, I'm a little clueless how all of this works, and I need to see if I can connect with you and Frank and make a few changes."

Dan's naturally suspicious nature resurfaced. "What kind of changes?"

"Nothing bad, you dick-twaddle. Now stop being a suspicious fuck and let's go over there and talk." She walked toward the building and Dan looked at John, who simply smiled.

Dan shook his head and followed Bethany Anne. She'd sure helped downtown when the police had their nuts in a vice. The FBI was still pissed off that some black ops group had gone through the "terrorists" like a hot knife through butter, leaving them with the dead bodies and nosy reporters' questions. Dan assumed Frank would kill the investigation soon by rerouting everyone who was investigating. No one could find anything out if no one was working the case.

He caught up with Bethany Anne as she asked the owner if she could use his office. "Not my office now, right?" the pilot said.

Bethany Anne retorted, "What, you think I want an office in here? You're crazy. I simply want to abuse your piloting skills and ride around in the Black Hawk."

Dan wasn't sure what he was hearing—was she buying the place?

She opened the office door and left it open for him to enter. It was a typical aviation office—mostly crappy furniture and piles of paperwork on an old metal desk with a fake laminate wood top.

She got right to the point. "So, how does this agency work? Do all you guys report to Frank or do you come in from the military?"

Dan ran a hand through his hair. Bill hadn't cared about how anything worked. He would arrive, get the op finished, and then leave again. Wham, bam, no questions, man.

Bethany Anne was a whole different kind of vampire. Yeah, maybe she did act more like a queen.

"We're seconded from different outfits. Some military, some agencies, depending on where Frank can pull them from and what experience they have. Like Scott having that Nosferatu experience up in New York. He couldn't talk about it outside a group like us who mess with it all the time. Until recently, it only happened a few times a year, so there were only two other dedicated team members and me. We've grown to the four core agents with a backup team, and the rest are support and medical. With you, I suspect we can get a little leaner, but I don't know if I'm comfortable with that, yet."

"What's a budget like this run? For all twenty-two of you?"

Dan sat on the incredibly uncomfortable chair. "That's the thing. We don't have one beyond the basics. We're a line item in the DOD, and it's so incredibly small it doesn't usually cause a problem with the bean counters. Carl had the big electronic tools that cost a lot, so we always leaned on him for that. You saw what we had in the field over here. Frank is able to provide the basics most of the time, but our living on twine and duct tape almost took us down last night. Why, you have an idea?"

"Yes. But I want your buy-in completely and unequivocally. If I don't get it, I won't go behind your back."

Dan's stomach eased a little. He knew how her own team

followed her, and she had a few others up north as well. Now, it looked like she'd hired a pilot with his own damn Black Hawk.

He decided he would be as open as he could. The vampire before him was nasty, scary, dangerous, and a handful. But she was also honest, fun, and a leader not afraid to deliver both asskickings and congratulations. She was what his team could get behind, and she didn't undermine her subordinates. In this case, him. "Let me know what you're thinking and let's see what we can work out."

Bethany Anne sat on the desk. She knew getting Dan on her side was a pivotal step in pulling her half-baked plan together. She didn't have a Stephen in America, so she needed to create an organization that had the connections, the muscle, and the manpower. Dan Bosse had done this for fifteen years. He had the background and experience she desperately needed.

"I bought this company here and a house in Smugglers Cove as a base of operations." Dan raised his eyebrows at that. She'd claimed to have spent what was his annual budget many times over. "But I need a core group of paramilitary men and women to create a strike force that can go on multiple simultaneous operations without a vampire. I won't always be available, and frankly, I'm not sure who I can trust at the moment. In the vampire realm, I can count them on one finger.

"I'm wondering if you would accept a change in direction. Frank will still be the government contact—or whoever comes after Frank—but I don't want to only handle issues he can help with. I want a worldwide organization we can depend on. We'll base it here and in the Keys to expand some of our capabilities."

"Where would we get the manpower?"

"Well, when you have one problem, it might be a pain to correct it, but if you have multiple problems, they might cancel each other out. What do you think?"

Dan's jaw dropped. He wasn't sure what to make of Bethany Anne's plans. But if she could make this type of organization work, he might finally feel they not only had a chance against the Nosferatu but could take the fight to them. Everywhere.

They decided to get Frank's thoughts on the subject and let Dan ponder it for a little while. He agreed to help on the first operation to set her plan in motion and go from there. She would catch up with Dan and the two persons of interest out in the van in a moment.

He left, and the pilot waved at him and headed for the office he'd just vacated. Dan had some thinking to do. He left the hangar and walked out into the light, catching John's attention. "Grimes! Come here, I need a report. What happened in the building?"

Bobcat opened his office door to find Bethany Anne sitting on his desk. He took the chair. "I see you're into something government-related. Do I need to know more?"

She smiled at him. "Better to not know if you get questioned, is that it?"

He smiled back. "No, I'm naturally curious, so I'm trying to establish the limits right up front."

She tried to decide how to explain he would sell his business and become the employee of a vampire. Michael hadn't covered this. She tacked it on to the other thousand things that bastard had failed to mention. If he didn't like the outcome, he could kiss her ass.

"Bobcat, I'm a full-disclosure type of person. If you're on the team, you're on the team. The problem is there is no 'off the team.' Not because I or anyone on my team would do anything to you if you don't talk. And trust me, we would find out if you talked. However, the 'other' team won't believe one word of your proclaimed innocence. They wouldn't have any problems simply grabbing you to see what you know if you aren't under my protection anymore. So, you can walk away, but you lose your protection, make sense?"

He scratched at his scruffy five o'clock shadow that was now going on twelve-thirty. "Was what you did back in town related to this?"

"No...well, I'm not sure. It could be, but it was pitched as a normal terrorist attack, so I don't think anybody who got involved on the spur of the moment will be targeted at all. So, you're safe there. You can step out of this office with everything you started with this morning plus the money I promised you— which has already been deposited into your account, by the way. I don't want you thinking I would hold that money back from you."

"What kind of upgrades were you thinking?"

"What can you fly?"

"Almost anything military, except fighter jets and nuclear bombers. Those, I could probably figure out if you aren't in a rush to get off the tarmac." He smiled when he said that. It sounded as if it was plausible he might be in that situation, so he should set a few boundaries up front. Bethany Anne returned his smile.

She considered the future and where they needed to end up. "Would you consider learning a new craft and perhaps teaching others when you've learned enough?"

"If they have the talent, sure, but I need to be the judge of the talent part. I don't mind a pilot risking their own necks, but I won't be responsible for rubber stamping someone so they can kill others with their flying."

"That's fair and what I would expect. What's your business worth?"

"Mostly debt. The lease on this space is up in six months, and with your fifty thousand dollars, I now have about fifty-seven thousand dollars in the bank account and a car note that will make you blanch."

She laughed at the car note comment. "Not if it means I get to keep you and that Black Hawk. Okay. Our new base of operations will be the house I just bought."

Bobcat barked a laugh. "You bought a house in Smugglers Cove, and you intend to run your base of operations from it?"

"Sure. It seems feasible that we can get some boats and leave from there. Wait until you see the boat I intend to buy. I'll send the team in if they have a minute and tell them to answer all questions truthfully. Make sure you feel you'll fit because I don't handle anything but the best relationships on my team. You really don't want me to kick your ass, so make sure you get along before you sign on the dotted line."

"Kinda like signing in blood?" He smiled as he said it.

She cocked her head and said, "Yeah, that's about right," and left.

Bethany Anne was walking out of the hangar when her phone rang. It was Nathan.

CHAPTER 17

**New York City, NY, USA**

Ecaterina worked with Nathan to get Nancy all the information she needed to close the deal down in Florida. He had a real estate company set up with a huge number of cutouts to hide who owned it. It might be something Bethany Anne would be able to use, but he didn't want to front her down payment on a nine-million-dollar acquisition.

"Bethany Anne? It's Nathan. Do you have a minute?"

"Sure. I presume this is about the house?"

"Yes. One of my businesses has real estate, and I use a bunch of cutouts to hide ownership. Namely me, in most cases. It takes a while to set up all these shell corporations. Do you have any desire to work with me on this?"

"Really? That would be fantastic. Hell yeah, let's do it. What do you need from me?"

"Oh, about 2.5 million dollars to handle the down payment." Nathan smiled.

"Why not the whole amount?" His smile turned incredulous. He'd forgotten she was stupid rich. He didn't know how rich, but Michael must have given her access to some serious money.

"Uh, yeah. We can do that."

"Nathan, can we use those corporations to hide additional purchases?"

"Like what, ten thousand pairs of shoes?"

"Hey, I'm not Imelda Marcos, you overrated mental amputee. I want to buy an aviation company that has debt from purchasing a Black Hawk, and I intend to spend a lot more as I get more toys and the upgrades I want on those toys."

"Good God, Bethany Anne. These are serious toys you're talking about." He made a mental note to not joke about vast quantities of shoes.

"Yeah, well, the other side isn't playing fair, and I don't have a problem cheating either. It's why I'm going to upgrade the toys."

"I should say you don't. What kind of money are we talking about?"

"Short term? Probably a hundred and fifty million dollars. Longer term? Probably six times that."

*Good God,* Nathan thought, *that's a billion dollars. Hang on, world, this just got really serious.*

"Yeah. I can make that happen, but I'll need to get your authorizations and signing ability on your accounts. Are you okay with this?"

"Sure. Just remember, the exit interview after misappropriation of funds is incredibly short and fatal and we're good."

"Never doubted it."

"Good to know. I'll contact Kevin Berger over in Zurich to get you on board. I'll see if he can make this happen or if I have to go back over there."

"No, they should have someone here in New York. But you *will* have to be here to do it."

"No problem. I'm coming up there with a team to deal with our recalcitrant puppies. Do you and Gerry have any ideas yet?"

"You mean ideas that don't end in mass slaughter?"

"Yes, those are the kinds of ideas I mean."

"Uh, no. This stuff has been percolating for decades, and some simply can't see the danger because they can taste change in the air."

"Yeah, they might taste change, but it'll be my foot shoved down their throat if they don't like it. Consider a way to get a conclave together of the biggest problem children whom you think are at least open-minded enough to talk without doing something stupid. I'll accept a truce for the discussion, and unless they do something completely stupid, they'll leave with their health intact."

"What might be considered 'completely stupid?'" He knew of a couple of vampires who needed very little to piss them off.

"So long as they don't act like they'll physically harm my team or me, then we're good. If they have strong and stupid types, they might want to leave them at home."

"What kind of team is this? Do you have more vampires? I understand from Ecaterina that Ivan is working with Stephen."

Damn, she should have mentioned to Ecaterina that she didn't want everything shared with Nathan. It wasn't that she didn't trust him, but she didn't want to share all her actions with Gerry and Gerry's contacts. Like Frank. "No, it's my team who works with Frank."

"So they already know about the UnknownWorld. Okay. I hope they don't get intimidated easily."

"Shit, Nathan. My team took out two Nosferatu last night and a bunch of terrorists today. I don't think they'll flinch because of a few mouthy meatheads with a bad attitude. One second." She covered the phone with her hand. It wasn't to stop Nathan from hearing anything, but it gave the illusion of privacy. "Hey, Darryl. Are you and Scott available for a few minutes to talk to Bobcat? He's the pilot, Bill. Yeah, a nickname. Let him ask you anything he wants and answer it all honestly or decline to answer it at all. Nothing is off the plate for me. Yeah, even that. I don't care; your choice if you want to offer it up. I need you to vet him as the team's primary pilot. Yup, I'm hiring or buying his company, so make sure you boys can play together in the sandbox, thanks."

She came back on the phone. "Sorry about that, needed to get some more discussions going while we talked. So, set up the meeting for us with the bank and with the hotheads too. I'll have an additional four with me. They will all be armed with silver frangibles."

"Bethany Anne, we both know you don't need support. There isn't a Were out there who can take you."

"It isn't about fear, it's about perception, Nathan. I don't want to scare them; I want them to want to join me. I won't ignore them since I want to co-opt them."

Nathan was speechless. This, he hadn't figured on. No vampire had officially worked with Weres or any of the Wechselbalg in anything other than a very superior position, but it sounded like Bethany Anne had different plans. She had brought humans in and called them team members. Certainly, she would do no less for Weres. Just what the fuck had Michael gotten them all into? He thought, not for the first time, that Michael was either a genius or a madman. Unlike the last time, he was smart enough to not say that out loud over the phone. While she couldn't scare the crap out of him like she had previously, he knew she would remember it.

He made some political calculations. Except for a couple of people on the Council who thought it was time to 'rise above it all and proclaim themselves superior,' this might work. He needed to talk to Gerry. He was the one whom this could seriously threaten.

"Okay, let me know if you need anything else, and I'll get together with Gerry on this. Anything special he should know?"

Bethany Anne considered this question. "No. Tell him nothing changes with the Council setup. I'll simply have a new organization that needs men and women who won't take any shit from anyone who isn't on my team. The Council will still stay in place

QUEEN BITCH

for everyone else. That should cover most of those who need an outlet for their more aggressive tendencies."

"Okay, I'll let him know."

"Great. My team and I will be up there tomorrow or the next day. Make sure you take care of Ecaterina as I'll pick her up and come back to Florida after the meeting."

"Will do. See you then."

They said goodbye and hung up. He moved to his laptop and went to sign in to the main database that showed where he had real estate in the Miami area. If he didn't already own any, he would go house hunting online. If the girl of his dreams had to live there, it seemed necessary to be able to visit her. He liked Bethany Anne, and he was sure he could visit her home anytime, but he didn't want to stay there and have her super-hearing listening in all the time.

### Miami, FL USA

Bethany Anne went out to the van, where Dan and John were still talking. They turned to her as she came up. John gestured with his head to the hangar. "What are the guys doing?"

"I'm having them talk to Bobcat, our pilot, to vet him. I still need you to do that if you have a minute after Dan."

Dan answered her. "No, we're finished. Nice piece of work. I have a team picking up that van you left over in south Miami. Don't want that left behind. Other than that, there wasn't much left for the FBI, and what you did to the team guarding the hostages wasn't seen very clearly. The only person I think had a good view was a mom who was watching her son as he was about to get beaten by that one terrorist. The one who lost his head?"

Bethany Anne nodded affirmatively. "Yup. He was about to slam his gun butt into the little kid. Fortunately, he was closest when I exited the stairs."

"Well, the stories coming from the hostages are that there

were at least two members on each side. One for each group of three terrorists."

"Are they still claiming it was terrorists?"

"The news isn't changing the story, so it's easier to call them that at the moment."

John interjected, "You guys need me? I'm going to talk to Bobcat and get this going. I'd be happy to have access to a Black Hawk and pilot all the time."

Both said no, and he went to join the rest of the team talking to Bobcat in the office.

"So, you were talking about the mom?"

Dan continued, "Yes. She saw you because she was already looking at that guy when you showed up and backhanded his head off his shoulders."

"Pretty much."

"Okay, well, she isn't talking. She has her son, and she wants to forget the whole experience. She's clammed up so tight you would think someone threatened her."

"Hey, it wasn't me! I didn't stop to talk to anyone. We had three minutes to get the op finished, so there was no lollygagging."

Dan snorted. "It took you guys maybe—*maybe*—one minute to take everyone down. Now, I find out from Eric that John seems to have excelled in the past twenty-four hours? Not to mention that he came back to me in perfect health after a massive knife wound and with blood all over him last night. Want to talk about that while I think about your earlier offer?"

Bethany Anne considered the situation. She wanted Dan on board, but she really didn't want this info leaked. "Yes, I'll share, but it will be on your honor that it never goes farther than you without my permission. That includes Frank as well, do you understand?" As she watched him consider her ultimatum, she realized she'd used that damn phrase "on your honor" that had started everything back with her dad at his base. She really hoped she wasn't turning into Michael.

"Agreed."

"Okay, take a walk with me." They started across the tarmac, and she didn't say anything for the first hundred yards. "How much do you know about how a vampire is transformed?"

"Not much. Bill didn't explain the situation except to say it's painful as hell and it's not easy to accomplish. The problem is that if you can't survive the transformation, you turn into a Nosferatu and you're little more than a hungry pile of vampire flesh without much intelligence. Cunning, yes, but not intelligent."

"True enough, I suppose, but the problem is that the way Michael and his children create vampires isn't the correct method. I won't go into the how and why of it right now. I *can* tell you that the first stage in the transformation is to correct any problems with the body at a cellular level. Nothing moves forward until that happens."

She waited to see if Dan could put it together.

"So, you're saying you had to give John your blood last night? Is that why you raided the blood stores before you left so fast to help them?"

"Not really. I needed the blood myself. My body converts it to a type of energy. When I got to the guys, they had taken out two Nosferatu, and John was bleeding horribly with his own knife stuck through his Kevlar jacket and a sucking wound in his lungs. I asked him if he would trust me. We had no time. He agreed, and I slit my wrist to feed him the healing properties in my blood. While I did this, Eric pulled the jacket and shirt out the way.

"When John couldn't drink anymore he fainted, and I dropped blood on and into the wound in his chest. I pretty much collapsed after that. Both of us were down for a while, and had just woken up when the helicopter arrived. By the time you saw John, the healing was almost finished. He didn't have enough blood to go past this first stage of healing, so worrying about him changing into a vampire is wasted energy. He can't do it."

"What about his new skills?"

"Honestly, I don't know what to tell you about that. I think it's only the first stage correcting some of the natural genetic mistakes in his DNA. If he hasn't told you, all his scars are gone now, and a problem he had with his calf is healed as well."

They stopped a couple of hundred yards away. Both gazed into the distance, lost in thought.

Dan glanced at her. "That's why you don't want people to know. You are literally the fountain of youth here in Florida."

She smiled. "Yeah, Ponce de Leon was a little too early to find me."

"Yeah, well, that was a fabricated story anyway. I appreciate you trusting me with this. I got your back, Bethany Anne. The fact that you would do that for John when you'd only known him for a few hours means a lot to me."

"Dan, they were my team. You don't leave your team behind, and letting them die when you can do something about it is, de facto, leaving them behind."

Dan made his decision. He held out his hand and she took it, confused.

"Bethany Anne, I am officially asking you to allow me to join your merry band of military miscreants as we fuck up these Nosferatu and anyone else who needs an ass-kicking across this world."

She gave him a hugely radiant smile and added, "And beyond the world, Dan? Any limitations?"

Little did Dan know what he was agreeing to. "No, ma'am. Whether they be here or anywhere out there we can reach, they will be dealt with."

She shook his hand. He couldn't believe this beautiful woman who had a smile to launch a million ships was as dangerous as she was. Dan finished the handshake, and they headed back to the hangar. It felt like he had started a major chapter. He would henceforth define his life as "pre-shake and post-shake."

He never did regret that handshake, but he often questioned his sanity at the time.

They called Frank together to pitch him on the idea and what was necessary to make it happen. He'd considered asking Bethany Anne to see if she knew how to give him a few years more. This was becoming fun again, and he didn't have anyone to give it to, anyway, now that she was batting for the other team. He consoled himself that he had been right and she would have made a perfect replacement for him.

Now, he had some arms to twist, favors to use, and suggestions to make. Life had moved past interesting to fascinating.

CHAPTER 18

**Miami, FL, USA**
Bethany Anne left Dan at the vehicle and decided to check in with her team and the status of her potential new team member. She paused and glanced at the Black Hawk. Up close, its dings and dents were visible with peeling paint in some spots. But there weren't any large oil leaks on the ground or around anywhere she could see. She wasn't a mechanic and didn't know what to look for, but she thought she'd be able to tell if it was a rattletrap. She wished she'd thought about its condition before they jumped on, but needs must, and she got really lucky.

She didn't want to trust luck again. Plus, she'd hired a pilot, first and foremost. They needed a mechanic on the team, and as far as she knew, they didn't have anything like that. She also wondered where the best place to store all her team's toys would be.

Flying around in a military helicopter was either over the top or rather infrequent. Since she expected to be running and gunning, over the top was the only choice.

Considering this, she walked over to the door and knocked. Eric pulled it open and peeked out. Seeing her, he opened it all the way and grinned. She smelled the alcohol before she saw the bottles the guys tried to hide from whoever was at the door and rolled her eyes.

She didn't want any, but she didn't care if they did. Since the five of them now acted like busted teenagers, she figured they were bonding just fine.

"Do I have to separate you guys from Bobcat? Is he already a bad influence on you?"

John pulled his Shiner Bock out from behind him. "Only if you allow us to keep his case of Shiner." He grinned unrepentantly as the others pulled their beers from their hiding places. Obviously, Bobcat had the best hiding place down under the desk since he sat in his own desk chair.

"You'd have to take that up with him. I suppose this is the ritual drinking of newfound friendship and team bonding?"

"We're all good if you're good. Uh, just one clarification?"

"What's that?"

"He's not sure he believes us about your, um…"

Bobcat took over. "Oh, geez, John. Grow a pair." He turned to Bethany Anne. "Are you really a vampire?" He didn't look concerned by the question, merely curious.

She smiled and willed her eyes to glow red and her fangs to grow. Bobcat looked a little shocked at the reality. It was one thing to talk about the pretty, intense team leader. It was entirely different to see what she looked like when she went all vampire on them. It took everything he had to not try to crawl into his right-hand drawer.

Her eyes returned to normal and her fangs retracted. She'd hated the idea of doing that back in Switzerland, but now realized it simply was the easiest way to make a point. Apparently, it affected the person looking at her at a fundamental level that triggered the fight-or-flight reaction. Always flight, though.

Bobcat took his cue from the guys around him. They weren't ready to fight for their lives, so he was able to pull his shit together. He didn't think his companions would steer him wrong.

He looked at the guys but talked to John. "Sorry about not believing you."

John laughed and put his hand out to shake. "Welcome to the team, Bobcat. If you can handle when our leader vamps out like that and not pee your pants, I think you can cut it. You got my vote."

The pilot leaned forward and shook his hand, then looked at the woman with the smile on her face. "Anything I need to do?"

"Well, I don't have an HR office, if that's what you mean, and I don't seal it with a bite either." She smiled, and the guys took the opportunity to laugh off a little tension.

"So, you're now my lead in all things having to do with transportation on the ground and in the air. I need to get the six of us to New York the day after tomorrow. I don't care how we get there, but I want it fast and safe. Also, do you have a mechanic?"

Bobcat shook his head. "Not full-time. Most of the basic engine work, I do myself. I've got a chief engineer friend who's between rotations and helps me from time to time."

"Is he good enough to retrofit the bird out there?"

"Like an engine overhaul? She shouldn't need that for another five hundred hours."

"No, I mean brand new engines. I want the latest available engine for that bird. While you're at it, see what the difference is for a new bird. I don't want to be penny-wise and pound-foolish."

"A new bird is probably north of thirty million."

"And new engines?"

"Not even close."

"Well, check into it. I suspect we will use you for drop-off and pickup, and maybe supply runs. No telling how bad it could get. Also, see what the latest coatings are—anything we can get that wouldn't be obviously military. We can't hide her during the day, but maybe we can put a face on her that hides her in plain sight."

"What, something like a changing paint?"

"Well, sure, if that's possible. I was thinking of something like a dark red that doesn't scream military during the day but is still hard to see at night. Plus, anything radar-absorbing to mix with it if possible."

"That will put us up the government's ass, you know."

"I'll let my government contact deal with that end. John, you and the team need to figure out what we need for an op in two days. We're going to meet a group of unruly Weres, and we need to look sharp and as badass as we can. Consider our dress on and off op. Dan's signed on to lead the new unified team, and Frank is on board to give everyone the chance to join me if you want to. If you want out, I'll understand. You guys didn't even know me before yesterday."

She looked them each in the eyes, and none doubted he was in the right place.

"Okay, I'll take it all of you are going with it?"

Scott said from the corner, "One for all and all for TQB!" All of them except Bobcat busted out laughing.

*Gott Verdammt*, she wouldn't get to change that name now. *Oh, well, make it your own,* she thought. "That's right, and you guys just became my bitches, so get your asses in gear. I want to be wheels-up by 5:30 in the morning day after tomorrow.

They left happy and excited. The team had feared Bethany Anne would move on to her other responsibilities and they would be broken up until the next event. Now the action wouldn't stop, and they finally felt like there was hope for the future and a way to take the fight to the enemy. They were still on their high from two successful ops in twenty-four hours, and they didn't want it to end.

There was one thing they were sure of. Around Bethany Anne, life would not be boring.

. . .

## Over the Atlantic between Miami, FL and New York City, NY, USA

Bobcat lifted off a few minutes after 5:30 AM with Bethany Anne's team and an extra co-pilot. She took a few minutes in private with John to discipline him for missing the planned take-off time.

He respected her point and took it for the team this time. But he received the message loud and clear that there was only one way to get things done, and it was his responsibility to make sure it happened.

She went to the cockpit of the rental Gulfstream G550. It was a pretty large jet, able to accommodate almost twenty passengers. For her team of four, it was overkill. She told Bobcat to rent it because she wanted to know if she liked it enough to purchase. Even with her extensive wealth, her toy list was damn expensive. She would need a way to somehow make some money from this. At least eventually.

That reminded her; she needed to discuss the future with TOM. Which meant someone would have to help her with the businesses she already had access to and those she would need to buy or create to complete the scientific advances needed to breach the Earth's gravity. SpaceX and two other companies were pushing the envelope with rockets and suborbital aircraft launch. That was nice, but TOM's capabilities offered a massive increase in ability over anything they had right now.

That was a decision she needed to worry about soon, but not on this flight.

She went into the pilot's cabin and sat down beside her newest team member. The co-pilot they had "rented" with the plane had gone to the back for a few minutes to give her some time with Bobcat. Terribly inappropriate, but who would tell on her?

"Hey, what do you think of the plane?"

Bobcat looked it over. "Nice. It's got legs which we might

need. Who's kidding? We will need them, I'm sure. But I don't know about buying it. We're renting this bad boy for just shy of seven thousand dollars an hour with me flying, so the bill should be about sixty thousand dollars for the trip there and back. Considering the heavy-duty weapons we have on board, I realize you didn't want to fly commercial, but damn, Bethany Anne, this big?"

"Hey, I wanted to check it out for a full team load, and I hope to come back with more than five passengers. Did your chief engineer take the bait?" Bethany Anne had told Bobcat to contact his friend Billy 'William' Stevenson and find out how badly he wanted another tour in the Sandpit. They'd decided a contract to retrofit the Black Hawk, now nicknamed 'Shelly,' was a good idea. They would see if he wanted to leave once he put his blood, sweat, and tears into the girl.

Someone on the team mentioned Bobcat treated the Black Hawk like he had treated his old girlfriend Shelly, and that story stuck. Then he made a tactical error and exclaimed Shelly was not an appropriate name for a Black Hawk. The more he bitched, the more the team gave him shit, until he realized he had cemented the deal himself.

Now, William was ordering all sorts of parts to modify Shelly, including the engine upgrades the Army used in the latest iteration of the Black Hawk.

"Yeah, he was happy for the opportunity and is looking forward to working on her and upgrading the engines. He loves these birds."

"So, you finally gave in on the name?"

"Had to. The more I fought, the more the guys found ways to bring the name Shelly into the conversation. It was a losing battle, and truth to tell, I started to come around and liked it anyway."

"Good. When we get back, you need to decide if William is the right guy for our team. We need a kickass aviation engineer, and I hope he's the right fit. I want one who has military experience. He will have seen a lot of the problems our birds might have."

"What, stress cracks from hard use?"

"No, bullet holes."

"Oh." That kind of put a period to that conversation, and Bethany Anne looked out toward the ocean and let her mind drift.

They needed to find another hangar location. The one Bobcat had was good for commercial customers, but not for her team. She had Dan take over the logistics since he would know best how to move the assets around. His knowledge and insight from his fifteen years running this team could be trusted.

However, the slower speed they were flying at helped explain why Michael's plane had those kickass military jets. When you were called into an op, speed was a requirement, not merely a "nice to have."

Fortunately, they were only testing the plane. There was a new G650 Bobcat had shown interest in. He'd said the wait time was a mile long, and Bethany Anne had merely smiled. She was sure it was, but money might be able to speed things up a little. Maybe she should talk to TOM. He might have some ideas on how to build a better jet. She considered that for a moment. Starting a small jet engineering company could provide what she wanted and create the perfect cover for the engineering efforts to come. With so much to do, she needed a bigger team. She would have to talk to Frank and finally, get in touch with her father.

She knew what Michael thought about reaching back into her old life, but she had already broken the rules so many times, starting with Ecaterina, what was one more? So much had happened in the past seventy-two hours that she felt like she was on a roller coaster with no stop in sight.

She stood and patted Bobcat on the way out of the cabin.

QUEEN BITCH

There was no reason to think in the cockpit, and the co-pilot didn't need to sit in the back.

She passed him and joined her team to plan the strategy for making an impression in New York. They called Ecaterina to confirm what she had set up and would pick up for them.

If nothing else, New York would be a blast. Now, if she could make it work, the roller coaster would have jets strapped to the back.

They got down to planning the nitty-gritty.


### New York City, NY, USA

Carl Corruthers, the executive driver, waited for his customers to land at JFK. He was stationed at a large personal hangar. That wasn't too strange. Often, people would park multiple planes in one hangar. That this one was empty could mean they were all gone. His brief indicated someone was coming into town for a few days and leaving again.

Carl had been told to take the baddest SUV the company had —a beautiful Chevy Suburban that had been modified by Texas Armoring Corporation. It was so plush inside that the two rear seats could actually lie back like those on a first-class flight. They even had the little tables that could come out for work or drinks.

He didn't know who it was he'd pick up, but he imagined it would probably be a wealthy client who had delusions of grandeur. Carl didn't care as he would receive an automatic tip for the whole trip. He would have a great check at the end of this gig.

Finally, a jet landed and seemed to head in his direction. Oh, mama. That wasn't a little turboprop. It was a beast of a private jet. One could buy a car instead of renting one of these for a few hours.

Maybe they *were* important.

He straightened a little. The jet rolled near the hangar but didn't go into it before stopping. The door opened, and the co-pilot was the first off. Then one of the biggest men Carl had ever seen came down the stairs and headed straight for him. He was dressed in a two-piece black suit and carried a ballistic nylon bag that clanked.

"Name?"

"Carl Corruthers."

"John Grimes. Pleased to meet you, Carl. Is this the vehicle we requested?"

"If you requested a special executive protection package Chevy Suburban, sir, then yes, it is. We can get shot, and no one will get hurt inside."

"Good. Open it up and let me make sure there aren't any surprises."

Carl was startled, but it wasn't a big deal. He popped the locks and John went through the inside while another guy dressed in the same style pulled a mirror and went around the base, looking under the carriage. He turned around to see an incredibly beautiful woman come down the steps. Dressed in a black pantsuit with a suit jacket over her top, she had a subtle flair that wasn't makeup, but it was mesmerizing. He noticed that all the passengers, including the woman, had shoulder holsters and pistols. Ah, hell, who was he ferrying around? They looked like they truly needed this vehicle. While it might be nice to get a great story, he couldn't tell anyone if he were actually dead.

His easy gig had turned a little worrisome.

## CHAPTER 19

**New York City, NY, USA**

Gerry stood toe to toe with the Alpha of the Denver Area Pack, Jonathan Silvers. Jon was as salty as they came and had spent a lot of his time up in the mountains on his ranch. He had a nice spread out there. Most of his pack was of the live and let live mentality. His son, however, was a prick of the highest order, and because Jon had a large amount of land, money, and influence, his son Pete felt he was important as well.

The problem was that Weres judged your importance for what you had personally accomplished. The only thing Pete had accomplished was revealing his ability to turn into a wolf. Unfortunately, two girls had seen him changing, and one had taken video with her cell phone. This shattered the strictures, and Jon now had problems with both his son and his Council lead.

"Jon, you hard-headed sonofabitch. If you can't get Pete to fix this mess, either the Council will have to deal with it or Michael's group will!"

"This isn't *your* son you're talking about, Gerry! Get off my case. Michael hasn't been seen in years, and the rumors all say he is dead."

Gerry wanted to punch something. "Those are rumors! I've talked to Frank, and we don't know that for sure. I don't need another massacre on my hands, and it isn't Michael we'll be dealing with. We'll face Bethany Anne, you cockeyed imbecile."

Jonathan turned around to try to cool down. Yelling at Gerry wouldn't accomplish anything. Gerry was predisposed not to back down in an Alpha argument, so Jonathan wouldn't win that way. Plus, if it got out of hand, Nathan Lowell stood over in the corner of Gerry's office. Jonathan was just lucky Nathan wasn't in his pack. He didn't really know if Nathan or Gerry would come out on top in a fight, but he had to respect any Alpha who handled Nathan as his second.

He turned back to Gerry, trying to keep his voice calm. "Look, I hear you. We have a new vampire here in the States, but you'll have to forgive me if I don't feel like believing she can be as vicious as Michael. That bastard was a cold-blooded and heartless killer. I hope to God he *is* gone, and good riddance. I'm not promoting that we reveal ourselves, but killing everyone who might make a mistake is too harsh. And that's what Pete's done. He's made some mistakes."

"So why can't he fix his mistakes?"

Jonathan's shoulders slumped. That was the root of the problem, wasn't it? Pete wasn't a mature guy, and when he made a mistake, he wouldn't own up to it. Everything was someone else's fault. It infuriated his father, so he hadn't dealt with it, and it could be the cause of Pete's death. He didn't believe the new vampire was powerful because he didn't want to believe it. He couldn't believe it if he wanted to hope his son had a future.

He looked up at Gerry and came clean. "Because I didn't do my duty to make sure he would be a stand-up man. I went to work on my ranch instead of my son. It was easier to give him a cherry sucker than a spanking, so here I am, worried that if you're right, I've killed my son by being lazy instead of keeping him alive with discipline." He was emotionally spent and sat down on the couch in Gerry's office.

Gerry didn't know what to say to that. This sudden declaration caught him off guard. He wiped his face and sat down in a chair between the couch and his desk. He put his elbows on his knees and rested his chin in his hands. "Nathan, you got anything?"

Nathan stirred from the spot where he had been all but holding up the wall. "I have little patience for Pete if that means anything. But if you mean do I have anything to help this situation, I'm at a loss. We have two women to whom Pete has shown himself changing from a human to a wolf. That's not only against the strictures, but it was also careless and stupid. Now, we have one video that thankfully, is mostly too dark since he was being an ass at night and she had a crappy cheap camera phone. Pete doesn't want to deal with the women anymore since he only knows how to put his head in the sand. The women are starting to think maybe they can make money with this. What a cock-up."

"What do you think Bethany Anne will do?"

It was Nathan's turn to wipe his face. "Well, I can tell you her first reaction isn't to snap someone's head off, but she doesn't suffer disrespectful fools either—which is just about the definition of Pete. So, I don't have much hope if we get her involved, but I don't know how to *not* get her involved. She has the ability to make this all go away."

Jonathan latched on to that comment like it was a lifeline thrown to him at sea. "How can she make this go away?"

Nathan looked at him. "Well, she can probably wipe the women so they don't remember, but she isn't really enthused about that option. She could wipe Pete back a few years and you could start over."

Jonathan went white when he realized how powerful she must be to accomplish wiping years of a person's memory away.

"She probably wouldn't want to do that either. She could also simply kill everyone—the girls, Pete, and anyone who pissed her off. I'm telling you, Jonathan, the best chance you have is what you just did, and that's to explain the problem and hope she sees a solution we don't."

Gerry hadn't expected to talk about Jonathan's kid. They were supposed to finalize the plans for the people they had termed the "green" team—as in, the guys were so green they didn't know enough to keep their mouths shut.

The Weres on the green team, however, thought it was a great name, and assumed it had something to do with a fresh start.

Either way, this conversation was derailing them. Gerry had only accepted Jonathan's appointment because he was an important person on the Council. "Jonathan, we need to finalize this meeting with Bethany Anne. The best idea, however, is to approach her with the problem. What do we have to lose? She'll be involved at some point, and it might as well be earlier when she has a better chance to help."

Jonathan relented. "Okay, I agree. So, what do we need to finish up this meeting? You're saying she agreed to a safe location?"

Gerry confirmed. "With the qualification that no one was too aggressive with either her or her team. If that happens, then she can and will take care of the problem."

"Is that why you left out Paul Gleason and his group?"

"Hell, yes. That hothead wouldn't be able to keep his mouth shut, and we would be knee-deep in blood in five minutes."

Jonathan shook his head. "He called and complained to me and others on the Council. How he was able to string together 'No Implementation without Representation' boggles my mind."

Gerry snorted. "Coached, I'm sure. There are players on the Council starting power grabs. This is a pain in the ass, and frankly, something we don't need. If we aren't careful, we'll have knives in our backs as well. I've been tempted to introduce them to Bethany Anne and walk out of the room. After a few minutes, I would simply just work with whoever she left alive." Gerry laughed darkly. "Still tempting, frankly. I understand she's in town?" He looked at Nathan.

"Yes, Ecaterina was picked up at my house ten minutes ago. She sent a text."

Gerry grimaced. He knew how much Nathan cared for Ecaterina. "That has to hurt."

Nathan merely shrugged. "She's not leaving forever, but the time I wasn't with you, I was with her. I'll fly down to Miami with them and close on a property I'm buying near Bethany Anne's little hacienda."

Jonathan asked, "Where's her house?"

Nathan smiled. "Smugglers Cove in Key Biscayne."

Jonathan looked at him. "Damn, that is one expensive *casa*. Really?"

He nodded.

Gerry looked at Jonathan. "How the hell do I not know about this place but my friend who lives on a ranch up in the mountains of Colorado does?"

Jonathan smiled at Gerry. "*Lifestyles of the Rich & Famous*. It's a sinful habit, I know, but I love Robin Leach's accent."

Gerry rolled his eyes. "Okay, fine. Let's get our own show going. I'll meet you guys downstairs at the car. You driving, Nathan?"

"Yeah, I've got the Benz, so let's use that."

Jonathan and Nathan left the office to go to the garage under the building. Gerry went to freshen up quickly and then joined them. He rode shotgun, and Jonathan got in behind Nathan.

---

Bethany Anne had selected an out-of-the-way place on the Queens Rockaway Peninsula, Fort Tilden, for the meet. It was a desolate area that had been used by the military for aircraft defense. She wanted to be away from New York City so the cops would take a while to get out there if things went bad, and also so that she had an escape route that wasn't the sewers of New York.

She expected somebody to be stupid. Although she only had four people with her, she hadn't excluded the other team. She'd persuaded Frank to allow the use of a couple of boats at a distance and a few small drones that couldn't fly above about a thousand feet. Still, with their 4k FLIR cameras, she should get a read on the situation before too many people got hurt.

She had asked Frank to capture as many faces for identification as he could with his promise they wouldn't be tagged in the database as Wechselbalg. Surprisingly, he was actually familiar with the term. It figured she would be the last to get the memo.

Her team was using the latest and best protective gear she could buy. Ecaterina had purchased everything in New York, a city that had access to almost everything legal and otherwise. Bethany Anne had made sure Ecaterina got it to Bobcat and the plane for safekeeping.

Frank couldn't give her overt military support for working against the Weres, no matter what he might want to do. Until they became a bigger problem, they were American citizens with their rights intact, not Nosferatu. At the moment, it was her game.

The five of them worked their way through Queens, heading out on the 278 to the 27 and finally, turned onto Oceans Drive. Bethany Anne realized why Michael ended up simply slapping the shit out of people. Trying to keep everyone alive when frankly, they were of questionable help, became a little harder each time she did it. Her patience was worn down, and she'd only been doing this for a short time.

What would happen when she was a hundred? How about two hundred? Would she become so impatient that making a book of sins that told you in black and white what was okay and

QUEEN BITCH

what wasn't became the solution? She had seen how well that worked for Michael, but it was hellishly tempting.

It wasn't the Stephens of the world who caused her problems. It was this situation with the Weres that got her down. She went into this meeting hoping for the best but planning for the worst. Not only from a tactical perspective but expecting the worst in people.

Her heart grieved because she expected to kill again that evening. She gave herself a pep-talk. If they acted on her request, no one would die. It was a huge step up from the normal policy of vampires. She fought from a superior position to facilitate equality of importance. There was no question of equality of strength. Between the wealth Michael had provided her with, Frank's help in the government, and her own abilities, it would be a massacre if she chose to go down that path.

But the woman who had gone into the mountains in Romania hadn't died. She still believed in giving others a chance. Unfortunately, everyone in the UnknownWorld played a higher-stakes game simply because of who they were. You didn't get to play by the paupers' rules when you were born into royalty.

If your race was responsible for scaring the bejesus out of humans for centuries, you tended to be very cautious. You sneezed wrong, and the pitchforks and flames came out. Except now, it was twelve-gauge shotguns, Molotov cocktails, and then the military would start firing guided munitions.

Carl cut over to Flatbush Avenue using Avenue J and crossed the Marine Parkway Bridge to reach to Rockaway Point Boulevard.

She had priorities that wouldn't change. As TOM had so helpfully reminded her, she was responsible for the future of the whole damn planet. More important to her, she was responsible for the team that was with her right now.

Bethany Anne sighed and reached into the cooler they'd brought along. Inside were five bottles of fresh blood. Her face showed her revulsion at drinking the stuff, but she couldn't have it with her inside the meeting. Fortunately, TOM had worked out the problems with the poisons that usually caused the nasty smell of death which hung around vampires. She'd asked him to squelch that. It wasn't vain of her to worry about smelling bad, right?

She drained two bottles and left three in the cooler. Eric provided a rag to clean her mouth. She appreciated the offer. By now, her personal team was aware she hated drinking the blood.

TOM hadn't found any solutions for pulling the Etheric-charged components out of blood that would help make the drink a smaller, more energy-concentrated liquid. Maybe she should find out which of Michael's companies worked with blood? She would bet at least one or more already did. She felt like she was behind on her homework.

Bethany Anne put her game face on. Carl drove through the gate to the meeting place, which was inside one of the empty concrete bunkers that opened toward the city and the sea.

The car stopped, and they waited in it. John spoke up after a minute. "Well, damn. I had expected our first attack to happen when the car stopped. There goes my fifty dollars."

Carl said in a squeaky voice, "What? When were you going to tell me this?"

"I just did."

"No, you didn't tell me anything. You merely informed everyone you lost a bet about us getting attacked right now."

"Keep your panties on. The next possible ambush is as we get closer to the meeting place. You'll be here in the car." John looked at Carl and got his attention. "Let me warn you that if you drive away, I will find you, and you won't enjoy the discussion. Do you understand this minor threat, or would you like me to escalate it?"

Carl shook his head. "I'm good. As long as you guys aren't in the car, I'll keep it locked. Not much can get through this armor."

"Very good." John opened the door and slid out. Making sure his weapons were ready, he walked around the car. Eric was next, followed by Darryl and Scott. Once they'd studied the grounds for a couple of minutes, they told Bethany Anne it was okay to come out.

They had decided treating her this way would work for the Weres. They understood two things at an instinctual level: power and respect. If you had the respect of the powerful, that was a level of power all its own.

Bethany Anne emerged from the SUV and sniffed the air. She could smell Weres, but nothing else out of the ordinary. It felt good to inhale salty sea air again.

John had speculated they would create burrows in the ground and jump up to ambush the SUV when they arrived. It was what he would do, especially if they believed Bethany Anne was a weak vampire.

Eric guessed they'd be hit right before they entered the tunnel. She was pretty sure that wouldn't happen, but without the protection of the armored SUV, they couldn't be nearly as blasé this time. The team formed up around her to make a point. While she was the deadliest of the five, they were there to protect her.

She sure hoped no one had considered shaped charges and ball bearings. That would put a damper on the rest of her life. She couldn't smell any explosives, so she was mostly sure they were safe.

They had changed out of their travel uniforms, which were the black suits, white shirts, and the underarm holsters. Now, they wore their ops uniforms. They looked very deadly coming down the hill from the parking area.

She had procured some ops helmets to provide them information in a heads-up display (HUD). The optical glass protected their faces and provided very small video views from cameras embedded in the helmet. They had their AR-15s on quick-slings with the same setup they used when hunting Nosferatu. All the ammunition they packed on this op was silver frangible and silver-laced. Even the Bowies had been changed out.

Bethany Anne had requested input from Nathan. She liked how the Bowie she'd used on Algerian was so effective at getting his attention. She had Ecaterina work with the craftsman Todd Thames. He didn't come cheap, and when you wanted five specially made knives within twenty-four hours? Well, let's say the quote would have choked most people. With lives on the line, she'd merely agreed to the price and provided an incentive if he was able to finish early.

She had hoped the Bowies wouldn't be necessary. However, she really liked the knife, and it was better to be prepared than not.

John and the team knew they were working against supernaturals, but they had been ground in the crucible of the Nosferatu for months now. They were brothers who had fought and survived, bled, and cried together. Now, John had a focus and a way to take the fight back to the sons-a-bitches who had attacked his nation. This meeting was a speed bump to moving onward to bigger plans.

If the werewolves talked, great. He was all for talking before fighting, but he wasn't worried long term. He had, almost literally, drunk the cherry Kool-Aid when Bethany Anne had saved his life. He realized his focus had shifted to her focus.

He didn't follow her blindly. He understood the mettle of the woman and trusted who she was, scary vampire and everything else. If everyone there talked, great. But the first asshole who did anything more than yell would get a beatdown.

Scott, behind Bethany Anne, had to watch his quarter, which included the area behind them. Both he and Darryl had their backward-facing cameras on their helmets. It had taken the team an hour to adjust to the technology on the flight up.

When Dan had approached Bethany Anne with the idea to use

the helmets yesterday as an option for the team load, she called and got the manufacturer's rep, who spoke to the both of them on a conference call.

Fortunately, the man had a distributor in the Miami area that had a case of ten of the helmets. She told him to ship them all via hotshot delivery, and Dan and Scott had worked with them last night and passed them to the team before they took off that morning.

Hopefully, adding this new gear wouldn't be a problem. They needed it because they didn't have the overhead support and other capabilities they usually enjoyed. The small drones were up there, somewhere. Frank was also online but wouldn't interrupt unless he had intel.

They spread apart as the team reached twenty-five yards from the opening, and all of them dropped sensors to help watch their back door. They approached the entrance which was twenty feet wide and ten feet high and examined it carefully. Nothing but concrete spray-painted with graffiti and gang symbols. Ricochets might be a bitch, though.

They walked through the entrance on their side of the bunker. No ambush occurred. Darryl and Scott had both lost their fifty dollars. It was now between Eric and Bethany Anne.

He believed they'd get hit right before they went into the tunnel. She'd chosen last and suggested something might happen during the talks. She knew Nathan wouldn't be involved in a double-cross. Not only would his life be forfeit, but he also wouldn't turn his back on Ecaterina. At least, that was how Bethany Anne read him.

So, that meant Gerry would play fair, and therefore the main meeting was on the up and up. She had a phone call with Gerry, Nathan, and another alpha they had in the car by the name of Jonathan. He'd raised a personal issue which they'd discussed for a quick minute. She said she would speak to him later, assuming they got through the talks.

The meeting had been set for 4:00 PM. At this time of year, Bethany Anne knew the sun would start to create long shadows in another hour. It should encourage the Weres' desire to get through the meeting quicker.

The general belief was vampires and Weres were stronger at night. Neither was really true. Bethany Anne knew the Etheric changes the Wechselbalg went through were equally powerful, night or day. Vampires were so secretive that no one realized this was also true for vampires. The team there might think she wasn't as strong as she could be in a few hours and would want to hit early.

Since Gerry and the main Council shouldn't be a part of any trouble, they unfortunately would be in the crossfire if not actively targeted. Or they could think it would be a wonderful time to strike while she was weaker. It was a calculated risk, either way.

Gerry, Nathan, and one more, whom she presumed was Jonathan, approached from the other side. She could see thirty to forty additional Weres beyond them. That group remained at the other end of the tunnel. The agreement, for the first part of the meeting, was that the main three representatives, Bethany Anne, and her protective detail talk in the middle.

Both sides agreed that if there was to be an ambush during the talk, this should entice them to spring it.

The headsets for the team included military-grade bone conduction technology from BAE Systems. This technology used vibrations that passed through the team's cranial bones and directly affected the cochlea. It allowed information to be given to the team and significantly reduced any chances of the Weres hearing their communications.

Frank's voice came over the comm. "We have movement. Ten incoming behind you, and I see a group of twelve joining the large group at the other end of the tunnel. That group is making their way through to the front. So far, that's it. Twenty-two tangos."

Bethany Anne knew all her team heard the message, but Nathan, Gerry, and Jonathan weren't in the game yet.

They had agreed during their conversation that if Bethany Anne's group was attacked from her rear, Gerry and his team would start the ball rolling and Bethany Anne's group would support him. If it got too nasty, she would get involved.

If the troublemakers started in on Gerry's side, then her team would initiate in support of the existing Council, and she would get involved with the first blood on her side again.

Unfortunately, she had to stay out of it until someone drew blood or was stupid enough to target her directly. She'd argued against these rules. Both John and Nathan insisted they played for bigger stakes this time, and she should be a little patient and trust them.

They closed to ten feet. She put her hand up to her ear while looking at Nathan and mouthed, "Ten behind me, twelve behind you."

Her team was already alert. Darryl and Scott had stepped over to the walls and knelt, ready to pivot and point their weapons behind them. John and Eric looked past the Weres in front and watched the group farther back. Bethany Anne's responsibility was for the group directly in front of them.

CHAPTER 20

**New York City, NY, USA**
Nathan caught Bethany Anne's message that twenty-two uninvited guests had joined the meeting. Her desire to keep the bloodshed to a minimum probably wouldn't happen.

He had studied the four tac team members in her group. He didn't know where she'd found them, but they were pretty fucking serious. Personally, he was glad they were there.

With only Bethany Anne and her detail present, more might try to join the fight, thinking to overwhelm her. He had finally decided Jonathan wouldn't turn on them. With the eight of them, it would be an interesting fight.

The two men behind her stepped sideways and dropped to one knee, ready to turn and support Gerry's group facing the other way. He imagined they also made sure no one in his group turned around. They were the guys responsible for protecting the team's back, and he didn't sense any hesitation they might have around a bunch of werewolves.

Gerry stopped five feet from Bethany Anne and looked at each member of her team, then at Jonathan and Nathan, and back at the vampire. "Plan B?"

## QUEEN BITCH

She sighed. "Yeah, looks like it. Sorry about the breakage. I tried."

Gerry smiled sadly. "I know. If we can keep it down to just the uninvited, we will have had a small victory. Unfortunately, I'm not sure you really would be able to make a good point without something like this happening anyway. I have to tell you, I'm happier being on your side than not."

Her smile lit up the tunnel. "You know, Gerry, that's the nicest thing you've ever said to me."

He looked perplexed. "Really? Where have my manners been?"

She replied, "In a sock drawer, probably." Bethany Anne looked at the other two. "Jonathan, nice to meet you. Nathan, you irredeemable nut-plonker, Ecaterina wants me to say hi." She smiled because whatever Nathan decided to say, Ecaterina would hear him back in the plane. Both she and Bobcat were in listen-only mode. Dan was as well, back in Florida.

Nathan merely smiled. "I'll see her soon enough, I'm sure. Did I tell you I'm buying a house in Miami?"

That busted Bethany Anne up. She laughed before getting her act together. What a way to woo a girl; let her know in the middle of an op that he was a stalky-stalker.

Then she heard Ecaterina's voice in her ear. "Tell 'friendly pooch' he better get his game mask on."

Bethany Anne leaned a little to her left to look down the tunnel toward the other group. It seemed like all the faces she could see in the front were ones she hadn't seen before. She leaned back again. "Well, it looks like this is about to start. Other than Ecaterina wanting me to tell 'friendly pooch' to get his game mask on, anyone got any last words?"

Gerry stifled a snort, and Bethany Anne could see that Jonathan, John, and Eric were all smiling. That was the result Ecaterina had probably gone for. Everyone was loose going into the showdown.

"No? Not you either, poochy-boy? Nothing, you got nothing?

Okay. Let's sit still until they kick it off. You guys got your ear protection?"

All three Weres casually put in earplugs.

"Eric, you ready?"

He brought his hand out of his pocket, showing her the flash-bang he had brought along. It had been Darryl's idea, and it was a brilliant one. Since Weres could increase their hearing sensitivity, he had suggested they might try to disorient them right away. Most of the "just frustrated" group would try to listen to the talk, straining their senses to the max.

The flash-bang would deliver a 170+ dB noise to rock their world, and since they would be looking into the tunnel, she hoped their eyes would appreciate the sudden eye-searing brilliance. Darryl caught Nathan's attention and tossed him one.

Bethany Anne grew impatient. "Well, fuck. What do these ass-wad badgers want? A fucking invitation?"

John smiled next to her. "Really? Ass-wad badgers? That's the best you got?"

"Give it a shot, you wanking crap-herder."

Jonathan couldn't believe his eyes and ears. This vampire was drop-dead gorgeous, but what an incredibly foul mouth she had.

Before John could reply, a voice screamed from behind Gerry. Everyone stilled, careful to keep watching their area.

"You won't let me join you, Gerry? I'm not good enough for the Council? Well, say hello to my little friend!" With that, the guy behind the voice raised an old Thompson machine gun.

Who the hell brought a Thompson submachine gun to a party anymore? What the fuck was this about? Before numbnuts could level his gun, Bethany Anne had already shot him twice in the arm holding the weapon, spinning him around before he fell on the ground. He was a big target.

She looked at John, who was exasperated with her as he asked, "Who was supposed to fire first?"

"Oh, don't give me any lip! He was quoting *Scarface,* for Pete's sake. Doesn't he realize what a dick move that is?"

John should have expected Bethany Anne to break the rules. Nathan noticed her team lead's irritation and smiled to himself. *Welcome to my world.*

Everyone continued their vigilance as Bethany Anne and her team lead engaged in a quick debate about following the agreed rules of engagement. Finally, the *Scarface* wannabe was able to stand and yelled, "Kill them all!"

*Well, that should cover the rules just fine,* she thought.

Eric let the flash-bang fly. Gerry, Jonathan, and Nathan took off toward their side of the tunnel while Darryl and Scott turned to cover them. Eric and John moved to the sides of the tunnel, and Bethany Anne simply dropped to the floor. There wasn't a good reason to stand at that moment. All of them shut their eyes.

Two of the new group heard the command and started to pull pistols from under their jackets. All the Weres were looking into the tunnel when the flash-bang went off. The enclosed space focused the sound. Many of the Weres dropped immediately, their hands over their ears, grimacing in pain. A handful fell to their knees and some didn't go down, but none were able to immediately start firing.

Unfortunately, Weres healed quickly from any sort of damage. Three of the twelve were already trying to fire blindly into the tunnel.

Bethany Anne heard the flash-bang go off on the other side of the tunnel.

She blew the brains out of the one in the middle while John stitched the one to the left up the torso. Eric put a three-round burst into the stomach of the one on the right. All three went down. Silver really made a Were lose focus.

Bethany Anne suddenly appeared in the middle of the group and the team went into action. She'd grab a Were, stab him in the gut with her Bowie, and fling him into the tunnel. John and Eric would catch the Were, who would be trying to deal with the sudden pain, and zip-tie them. John popped one on the head when he tried to kick him.

The last Were on the ground before Bethany Anne was Paul Gleason, the *Scarface* wannabe. Gerry had given her a quick synopsis of the possible party crashers and Paul, with his challenge, had been the obvious ringleader. He was also very easy to recognize from Gerry's description.

Everyone else had taken a step back, leaving Paul and Bethany Anne alone.

His arm had healed. He was at least three hundred pounds of muscle and fat, and his arms were huge. She wondered if she could simply arm-wrestle him for the win?

"You cunt-licking bitch!" His face was flushed red with anger.

Apparently not.

Paul heaved his prodigious weight off the ground. It figured she had to fight a Were who was as strong as a fucking ox. He had some blood draining from his ear, though.

She heard a shot and Eric yelled at one of the guys behind her, "I told you to fucking stay still! Now you get to feel that shit until we unzip you. Don't be a fucktard. We're trying to get you all through this without killing anyone, asshat."

"Stay down, Mr. Gleason. I'll only ask you politely once."

He continued to scramble to his feet, holding his Thompson in his left hand. She let him stand. *Might as well make an object lesson out of this one*, she thought. Most of the other Weres who had been hurt by the flash-bang had healed. Two in the front of the blast had a couple of friends trying to help them out of the line of fire.

She heard Darryl and Scott each fire. It must be entertaining back there as well.

Paul simply had to get his idiot on. He screamed at Bethany Anne again, spittle flying. "I don't give a rat's ass what you want, bitch. No vampire is going to take away my rights!"

He dared her to do something—anything. He was about a foot taller than her, and more than twice her weight. Paul had bested eighteen other Weres in fights and had downed twelve humans in a bar fight back in his hometown. She didn't look like she could hurt an old man, much less him.

One issue with fighting big or obese people was that it took a huge amount of strength to actually hurt them if you punched them in the stomach. Part of the problem was how much distance the punch had to travel through fat to reach the stomach before it could hurt them.

She was trying to keep this as death-free as possible. If she killed Paul, others would use it as a political tool for years.

Bethany Anne pivoted on her left foot and kicked him in his right kneecap, shattering it, and his fibula broke out of the skin. Paul hadn't seen her move. He went down again, and the Thompson dropped to the side. Now his cussing gained considerable volume. She walked over, picked the Thompson up, and considered breaking it. What a waste that would be.

She looked at everyone standing there. Then she strode over to Paul and looked down at him.

"Which part of 'don't stand up' didn't you understand? I personally don't give a shit what you say around anyone in the Were community, but if you let the humans know about the UnknownWorld? I will kill you, Mr. Gleason. Or, if you're man enough, you can try right now. How about it? Are you brave enough without your twenty-one other goons to take on the little-bitty girl vampire?"

At this point, Bethany Anne's patience broke. *Fuck 'em.*

Everyone who watched her face took one or two involuntary steps backward. Three guys in the rear turned and ran. Paul looked into Bethany Anne's face as her eyes turned red and her fangs grew out. He couldn't think straight anymore. She wasn't a tiny, frail woman. He began to pull himself backward and away from her in fear.

She reached down and grabbed his left leg, the one not trying to mend itself. Her voice was dark and deadly. "Come with me." Paul grabbed at the ground and at sticks, holes in the concrete, or anything else that might offer purchase. He struggled, kicked, yelled, and cursed as he tried to break the vampire's grip on his leg. She merely kept hauling him down the dark tunnel.

John watched as she walked forward relentlessly. He could see her eyes glowing in Bethany Anne's outline. That was fucking cool.

He and Eric had already dealt with the eleven guys who'd been stabbed, taken all their weapons, and triple zip-tied them.

One idiot had decided to show how Weres could huff and puff and break the zip-ties, so Eric shot him in the gut and zip-tied him again. He moaned in pain and sweated like a sonofabitch.

They sat with their backs against the wall and watched as the tiny vampire pulled the kicking and screaming Paul Gleason down the tunnel, all heads turning in unison.

She tossed the Thompson to John and kept moving.

Eric looked at him from the other side. "He is a cluster-fuck experiment."

John laughed. "Hey, if she didn't hear that—"

They could hear Bethany Anne yell over Paul's sobbing cries, "I heard that." She was halfway to the other entrance at that point.

John smiled. "Dammit! That was a good one!"

---

Nathan, Gerry, and Jonathan hurried toward the other entrance. They saw Bethany Anne's people pivot to aim up the tunnel. Jonathan sure hoped they were good shots.

Jonathan had gone to Gerry with mixed emotions. He had a really good idea of what would go down. He wasn't sure what he

QUEEN BITCH

would do, but he thought his only choice might be to try to kill the vampire. If he didn't, he feared his only child would be executed.

Pete was stupid, immature, spoiled, and a list of other things, but at the end of the list, he was still his son. He felt so much guilt for bringing him up so poorly. What he hadn't counted on was a vampire he could actually talk to. In the car, he decided staying with the Council and trying to make this work with Bethany Anne was the path he would take. She hadn't promised him anything other than that they would talk after this incident. Gerry had confided to him earlier out of Nathan's hearing that Nathan had told him he would leave before taking sides against her.

On the phone, she'd seemed…human? Well, good enough. She didn't seem like the cold, aloof vampires he was familiar with. God knew if it had been Michael, he would have tried to hide Pete. If his son didn't like it, well that's what drugs were for. Maybe by the time he figured where his dad had shipped him to and how to get back to America, he would have grown up a little.

Jonathan had allowed the rumors of a weak vampire to influence his actions. As he ran with Gerry now, he realized there were a lot of Weres who had also expected as much.

He was surprised at how collected she looked with the SpecOps team. This lady had been there, done that, and didn't give a shit what you thought. She only cared that you could walk the talk, and the men around her had obviously been able to do that. They seemed like a well-oiled team. But Nathan had told him she'd arrived in the States only a few days before.

How she'd gotten this team was a mystery to Gerry.

As they ran, he saw the flash-bang fly ahead of them. They heard the other teams' explode and closed their eyes. Everyone stopped running and bowed their heads and covered their ears. A second later, the flash-bang went off.

They finished the run to the tunnel entrance, and he heard the two humans come up the tunnel. Eight of the ten Weres were on the ground, trying to recover from the pain of the flash-bang.

The two still standing had their heads in their hands and were cussing.

The three formed up, with Gerry in the lead. He had to wait a little while for them to collect themselves.

Gerry yelled at them. "What are you idiots doing here? You were not invited by the Council to be a part of this conclave!"

The two guys who had remained standing puffed their chests out belligerently. The one on the left pointed back into the tunnel. "We aren't just going to let some vampire command us anymore!" His "more" was punctuated by a shot farther down the tunnel and someone from Bethany Anne's team telling another someone to not be a fucktard.

Gerry didn't look behind him. "And how exactly are you going to stop her?"

Both pulled pistols out of their jackets. The one on the right yelled, "By shooting the bitch, right, boys?" He turned to look at the other eight. They were all staring at him as Scott shot him in the head. He fell like a puppet whose strings had been cut.

At the same time, Darryl shot his partner in the stomach. It would hurt, but he would come out of it okay. The first one? Probably not.

Gerry shook his head and kicked the pistols behind him.

The eight still standing realized they weren't only facing Nathan Lowell— everyone knew him—but the Council leader, another alpha, and at least two shooters in the darkened tunnels.

They were officially screwed, and they knew it.

Their emotions told them to rip and tear and scream their rage, but under the hard gaze of the alphas, their desire was to submit.

Conflicting feelings roiled in their bodies and minds when they heard Paul Gleason crying and yelling and screaming in fear. He was getting closer.

## QUEEN BITCH

They peered into the tunnel. Even Gerry, Nathan, and Jonathan glanced over their shoulders. They could see Bethany Anne's outline moving closer and then the red eyes staring at them as she dragged Paul Gleason behind her as if he was a small sack of flour she pulled by a cord.

The closer she got, the more his sobs of pain turned to cries of fear as his knee slowly healed. They could tell his right knee had been messed up pretty badly.

She dragged him toward the two Council members and Nathan. Her voice dripped with malevolence. "You have a pack member who requires punishment. You can do it, or..." At this, she looked at the eight standing on that side of the tunnel. "I will take my punishment out on everyone I feel has broken faith with me today." She looked back at Gerry. "What is your decision?"

Gerry felt all eight of the standing pack pleading with their eyes for him to make a decision. The gut-shot guy on the ground looked at him, his fear overcoming his pain, and he shook his head as he held his arms over his stomach.

Gerry looked at Jonathan, who nodded. He then glanced at Nathan and nodded. Nathan was the one he relied on to keep his pack in line. No one liked it when Nathan Lowell came to town.

Nathan went over to Paul Gleason and told him to stand. Paul found his feet, his right leg now almost healed, and turned toward the Alphas.

Now that the vampire wasn't dragging him, he tried to figure out how to get out of this situation.

He wasn't happy, but he was in a tight corner. It was obvious that the group of guys who all wanted to "slay the vampire, let werewolves be free" were cowed by the circumstances and wouldn't do him any good. Gerry had never liked him, and Jonathan obviously licked Gerry's ass. Paul quickly forgot his earlier fear and a belligerent look crept onto his face. Everyone was watching him.

"What, you want me to apologize? Want me to say I'm sorry

for what all of us want, Gerry? We just want to be free, like we should be. Should I apologize for that?"

He almost believed he could turn this around and played to his audience again. He had stirred them into a frenzy on the way over here, worked them like a comedian played a room at Caesar's Palace. More confident now, he began his rhetoric again, willing the guys to anger once more.

"No little fucking cunt…" That was all he said before his head exploded, splattering half the belligerent group with his brain matter. Two had their mouths open at the time.

All of them looked at Bethany Anne, who hadn't moved. Damn! They knew vampires were fast, but— She merely looked up in exasperation and pointed toward the tunnel.

Their eyes and heads followed the direction of her finger to the tunnel entrance where Darryl and Scott stood. They both lowered their weapons. Darryl told them all, eyeing each one and making sure to include Gerry, Jonathan, and Nathan, "You *will* respect the Queen Bitch."

Scott added his own comment. "Or we will kill you. Do you have any questions?"

Even Nathan shook his head left and right. These humans were scary fuckers.

Bethany Anne walked back into the tunnel. "Let's get this show on the road. With all this blood everywhere, I'm getting hungry."

Two of the Weres shuddered involuntarily. She winked at Darryl and Scott as she passed them, and her eyes turned normal as her teeth retracted.

She hadn't killed Paul, so how upset could John be this time?

CHAPTER 21

**New York City, NY, USA**

The actual conversations after the fight were a little subdued. No one felt inclined to piss off the vampire or her guards, and they needed to get out of there. Gerry had already detailed a team to handle the bodies. He had been prepared with four windowless vans. He only needed one.

John and his team cleaned up all the bullet casings while Bethany Anne heard from those who had legitimate grievances with the strictures as they were now.

She admitted she didn't know where Michael was, and would probably pardon some of the harsher sentences and take the punishment for doing so should he show up.

Everything would go through the Council, and if anyone got ahead of her and took advantage of her "good nature," she or her team would implement the harsher sentences for breaking faith with her. If they had any questions, they could ask their Alpha, and their Alpha could ask the Council. The Council could contact her through Ecaterina.

Someone asked how they could get hold of Ecaterina, adding

that rumors were she was a really pretty woman. Nathan stood and eyed the guy and simply said, "Through me."

That brought the tone down a notch until Bethany Anne slapped his arm. "Don't forget, she's still listening. Do you want to make sure that works for her?"

Everyone laughed when they realized Nathan's face had lost a little color. Shit, shit, shit! "Of course, I merely meant as a preliminary process to be clarified later."

Sniggers were heard in the back of the group. No one wanted to piss off Nathan Lowell—except, apparently, the vampire.

The human John Grimes was beside her, but the other three faced outward, looking for additional danger.

Finally, they wrapped everything up and needed to go. They would schedule another meeting in the near future without so much drama attached to it.

The twenty uninvited Weres who were not dead or in a coma received a personal visit from Bethany Anne. With red eyes and fangs glistening, she asked each if they would abide by the Council's commands. It wouldn't be her problem unless they acted up again. She let each one know they had just received their only warning.

Her team walked back to the Chevy SUV and got in, and Carl took them back to the airport.

The plane wasn't the coziest to sleep in, but it was safer than a hotel, and they didn't have to deal with questions about the explosives and guns they had with them.

The next day, Bethany Anne wore a dark red dress and matching Blahniks to meet Nathan at the bank. Ecaterina went with her, and the vampire opened two new accounts. One she shared with Nathan so he could use it for withdrawals, and the second with Ecaterina, who opened a personal account as well.

She wasn't sure what to do about a salary for Ecaterina. It wasn't fair to keep her without her own means of support. She deposited twenty thousand dollars into her personal account, and told her they would work out her salary in the near future.

She then deposited one million into the account shared with Ecaterina to prepare the house in Miami. She placed fifteen million in the account she shared with Nathan. The house required ten million, and she needed money to start the process of purchasing Bobcat's business. Once they had all the details on the loan for the Black Hawk, they would pay that off directly.

She let the two of them enjoy lunch together while she went shopping for a pair of Christian Louboutins. She found a style at Neiman Marcus that almost matched a pair she used to wear to work all the time. It was amazing how much personal service you could get at that store.

She had them FedEx one of the shoes in a box with no return address to an austere-looking office building in Washington DC, and the other to a military base in Denver, Colorado. The sales lady never even blinked at the request.

Finished with sending her private packages, she caught up with Ecaterina and Nathan.

They actually kissed each other goodbye in front of her. Wow, her two little lovebirds were finally admitting to the world that they were an item. Ack. She could gag, but she was happy for them.

Nathan would follow them the next day. He had a couple of things he had to do in Boston in the morning before he flew down to Florida. Jonathan, however, had asked if he could have a seat on the plane. They talked, and she agreed. It wasn't like she didn't have space, either on the airplane or at the house. After a quick phone call to John, he agreed to the request as well.

Carl finally dropped the two of them at the airport and they said their goodbyes. Bethany Anne and Ecaterina had eight shopping bags of stuff at their feet. She noticed a sullen young man next to Jonathan. Guessing this to be the recalcitrant Pete, she walked over and offered her hand to Jonathan. John Grimes was there with him.

"Good afternoon, Jonathan. How are you?"

"Doing fine, Bethany Anne. I would like to introduce you to my son, Peter. Peter, this is Bethany Anne."

She looked at Pete, who merely raised his head in a gesture of "I see you." Jonathan frowned.

Okay, time to set up an object lesson.

Bethany Anne said, "Pete, you see those shopping bags back there?"

Pete snapped, "Of course. I'm not blind."

"Good. Then you won't have any problem finding them, will you?"

"I'm not going to be looking for them, so I won't have to find them." Pete's smirk was growing.

Jonathan evidently recognized what was going on. He almost said something, but caught the barely perceptible head-shake Bethany Anne gave him.

She closed the lesson. "And why would you think you aren't going to go get them?"

"Cause I'm not your slave, cunt." The next thing he knew, he was hit so hard in the jaw that his arms were flung to the side and his whole body went down. He hadn't hurt this bad in forever. When he started to focus again, it was the face of John Grimes in front of him.

"Listen, you little spunk rag. The last person who was disrespectful to Bethany Anne had his head shot off by my men. Be thankful it was only my fist that hit you. Unless you want an ass-whipping in front of the girls, you will get up off your useless ass and move those packages *gently* onto the plane. Then you will find a seat and be the nicest gentleman you can possibly be. Do you feel me, Pete?"

He looked up into the eyes of the human and understood this man wasn't his father. He would absolutely kick his ass if he didn't get into action. He looked for his father. Why wasn't he protecting him? Where was he?

He felt a tap on his shoulder and tried to roll his head the other way. His father would fix this asshole!

Jonathan's face finally came into focus. "Pete, you better listen up. I watched Paul Gleason get his head shot off for calling Bethany Anne names. She didn't kill Paul, her protection team did. You have to grow a pair and stop being a jackass. She will solve the problem with the two women back in Colorado, but you have to stay for three months with her team. I've not been promised you will come back alive, you understand me? Don't fuck this up, son." His dad stood, and he and Bethany Anne walked toward the car. Pete watched him reach the vehicle, where Bethany Anne spoke to him for a moment. Jonathan climbed into the car and left the airport.

His life was screwed up now for sure. Oh, my God, he was with the Queen Bitch herself.

Grimes grabbed him by the jacket and pulled him up. "Get your punk ass over to those packages and don't scratch any of them."

Pete was about to mouth off again, but his jaw hurt too much to talk right then. A good thing, he decided.

He walked sullenly over to the packages.

"Walk straighter. You're not a weakling, are you, Peter? Are you so frail you can't stand up straight?"

Peter straightened his back. Frail? Who the hell did this guy think he was? Peter would show him.

John Grimes watched him take the packages in two trips. His back remained straight and arms out, showing him he could hold the weight of the packages easily.

He smiled a little to himself. *Maybe the boy has potential,* he thought.

In Colorado, two women were each mailed envelopes with scandalous information they didn't think anyone knew about them. If they ever tried to say anything about Pete, the information would be released.

The girls discussed their situation and decided they weren't sure what they'd seen with that guy and the wolf, but they sure as hell didn't want the other information going out on their social media accounts. They both decided to delete the video and never talk about it again.

### Miami, FL, USA

The team made it back to Florida with no issues. Most of them went off to settle into the new digs, and Bobcat went over to his hangar.

His friend Billy "William" Stevenson was tightening a cover on his baby when he got back. They slapped hands and punched each other.

"How's it going with my baby, here?" Bobcat went into his office and grabbed two beers, offering one to William.

"Oh, you mean Shelly?" William smiled at Bobcat's grimace. "She's good. You've done all right by the old lady. How did your trip go?"

"About as smooth as we could have hoped. Not too much breakage."

William raised an eye. "Was that the glass type or the Sandpit type?"

"Sandpit."

"No shit?"

"Not a bit."

Now William was interested. He had wanted to be with an outfit, but the only chance to be with a group that was making things and breaking things was over in the Sandpit. If there was an option closer to home, he wanted to know more.

"Is that why you have me getting Shelly dressed in the nicest clothes I can find?"

## QUEEN BITCH

"Could be. But the answers you want are on a need to know basis, my friend. Not to be an ass, but unless you're interested in sticking around, you don't need to know."

William thought about it. He'd heard the stories over the last week about how a Black Hawk had been seen above the Southeastern Financial Center during the terrorist attack. Then it had landed in a park and a deserted field and finally, over in the ritzy Smugglers Cove area. He had put two and two together when he cleaned out some long grass from the landing gear—the kind of grass you might find in the area by Key Biscayne.

He had seen the hard cases coming off the G550 when they landed, and had a really good idea the black nylon ballistic bags weren't for golf clubs. He'd also watched a sullen teenager carrying shopping bags from expensive stores. His face broke into a smile as he realized it fit with the stories from earlier in the week. The Black Hawk was rumored to be above the building of the terrorist attack, and then only a couple of hours later, it was rumored that an eccentric woman was playing Rambo over in Smugglers Cove. She had landed her helicopter and bought a home right on the spot. A really, really expensive home.

William looked around Bobcat's office. "Did you say you're selling your business?" He took a swig from his bottle.

Bobcat merely smiled and took a sip of his beer. "Mmhmm."

"So, your new boss. Is she new in town?"

"You might say that. Why?"

"Just curious. If you had to drive over to where she lives, might you take the 913?"

"I probably would, if I wasn't flying Shelly over there."

That was about as close to the truth as William would get out of Bobcat. Sum'bitch. This was the team who took out the terrorists and bought a nine-million-dollar home immediately afterward.

"It doesn't look like these two helicopters would need me full-

211

time after the retrofit if all you're doing is flying around the Keys."

"I didn't say we would only have a helicopter or two, did I?"

"What else?"

"What else are you willing to work on?"

Ah, there was the question Bobcat wanted William to answer. They had shot the shit so many times the pilot had a good idea of everything William could work on, which was basically everything the Army had thrown at him in the last fifteen years. The question wasn't what he could do, but what he would be willing to do for the team.

"For the right reasons, I'm willing to put in all the sweat and ingenuity I got. My birds don't drop and my autos don't stop, but I won't do anything against my brothers, you know what I mean?"

Bobcat smiled. "I know what you mean. You interested in sticking around?"

William smiled. "Hell, yeah. The honeys are good on the beaches in Miami. That's a good enough sandpit for me. As long as I won't be bored, whored, or floored, I'm good."

"Trust me, the Army whores you out more often than Bethany Anne will, and you get floored every time you drink too much. You start a fight. You can't hold your liquor to save your life. As for bored? Well, it's for me to make sure that doesn't happen."

"Boy, I hold my liquor like the Hoover Dam holds water."

Bobcat busted out laughing, and William soon joined him. It was well known that while he could possibly drink a few beers, he couldn't hold whiskey down worth a damn. He would get belligerent and start a fight over whatever was popular on the news at the time.

One time in Texas, he'd had a couple of shots and stood up on the bar and called all the women in the bar his "hos," and the fight was on. They found him asleep under a table. As best they could work out later, he swung at the first guy who came at him and got decked hard enough to go down.

He would say it was good times, but he honestly couldn't remember any of it.

Bethany Anne had told Bobcat he needed to vet his chief engineer and was ultimately responsible for his actions. If he made a wrong decision, the exit interview could be a bitch.

Bobcat got the message. He would make sure William was the right guy before telling him too much. He didn't want to find out he was the cause of an untimely death.

### Miami, FL USA

A week and a half later, Bethany Anne was finally enjoying the house after three truckloads of furniture had been delivered.

Her neighbors weren't too happy with her. They had heard the story about her playing Rambo in the attack helicopter and thought she was a little too weird for them. On top of that, she had so many people living in her house, the stories had begun to fly.

The next-door neighbor bitched John out one morning because a work truck had blocked her driveway the day before. Bethany Anne was in bed and heard this lady shouting. She didn't appreciate that her neighbor was disrespectful to her team leader, or the yelling either.

She threw on a pair of jeans and a t-shirt without a bra. One thing the genetic changes provided was outstanding lift with no support necessary. Her not having to wear a bra made Ecaterina jealous.

Before becoming a vampire, Bethany Anne hadn't been very big in the breast department. She had been able to choose between bra and no bra, depending on the event. If she were human now, the no-bra option wouldn't have been on the table.

She walked down the driveway and out through the gate to

come up behind John, who was stoically taking this woman's abuse.

"And I'll tell you another thing. I don't know why you people have to be up all times of the night. It bothers my cat Mugsy dear to have to sleep with the lights coming over the wall. This was a pleasant little area before you moved in."

John straightened, his eyes looking like they were caught in a car's headlights. Bethany Anne stood behind him and had grabbed him around the waist in a very affectionate manner.

"Why, Ms. Joshwood. What an unpleasant surprise to find you being so rude to my friend John here. What are you bitching about this morning?"

*Oh, God*, John thought. He just wanted to leave in any direction possible. He had never liked being in the middle of a catfight. Then he remembered. *Shit, this woman is a vampire, so what am I worried about? The fact that she has her arms around me? That could be it.*

Ms. Joshwood saw a chance to start in on Bethany Anne. "Oh, you tart! How dare you complain about my complaining! Before you moved in, this was a decent street. We never had any trouble at all. Why can't you keep it down, and why do you have so many people in your house?"

Bethany Anne smiled at her. "Ms. Joshwood, you realize my house has nine bedrooms in it, right? Certainly, you understand I might need to try out every one of those bedrooms with John here before I decide which one I'll use for guests? Doesn't he look like a poster boy for virility to you?"

John's face turned red, then white, then he started looking like he might faint.

Ms. Joshwood, on the other hand, sputtered her indignation. Bethany Anne looked up at John. "Sweetie, would you be so good as to get Pete started on his morning calisthenics?" She patted him on the butt as he left and suppressed a smile as his back went ramrod straight and he hurried away as fast as pride allowed.

When she saw him go around the corner, she turned back to Ms. Joshwood, who was still trying to form a coherent sentence.

Bethany Anne's voice went silk over steel. "Ms. Joshwood, you are a pain in my ass. You will go talk to your husband and tell him you wish to move closer to your kids. Then you will put your house on the market to be sold for five hundred thousand dollars more than what your real estate agent tells you to list it at. I want this done within two weeks. Now get out of my sight, you fucking crone."

With that, she turned and walked back into her tiny estate, the black gates closing behind her. At least her fucking walls went around her house.

Two weeks later, she bought the house next to hers for 8.7 million dollars.

*FINIS*

LOVE LOST

The Story Continues with book 3, Love Lost.

Available now at Amazon and on Kindle Unlimited

# AUTHOR NOTES: MICHAEL ANDERLE

Thank you, I cannot express my appreciation enough that not only did you pick up the second book, but you read it all the way to the end, and *now*, you're reading this as well!

I mentioned in the *Author's Notes* at the back of *Death Becomes Her* that it took a while to write the first book. This book took a week. (I hope the quality is up to snuff) I won't get the third out in nine days, I guarantee it!

However, I do hope to have the third one finished and ready by 12/15/2015. That will accomplish having three books available, and I feel like I can afford to advertise at that stage.

Part of the reason (I think) I wrote this story so fast was I joined NaNoWriMo. Just that one step encouraged me to dig deep, and I jumped ahead. The second is that Bethany Anne is just a fun character to write about. Her experiences are almost as surprising to me as to my readers.

That whole Stephen episode was *not* what I expected at all. At the end of the first book, I expected Bethany Anne to find an annoying son of Michael who deserved a horrible beating for being an ass. I think I was literally writing the point where she hears his footsteps coming to the door when it jelled in my brain

## AUTHOR NOTES: MICHAEL ANDERLE

that Stephen was old…really, really old. Now, he's my second favorite character.

I mentioned on a recent blog post that an author's success usually entails *lots* of pre-work before you release your book. However, I just put *Death Becomes Her* out in the wild with no notice and no advertising. I really hope that if you enjoy reading these stories, you will share the link with your Kindle friends and encourage them to read it as well.

As far as I can tell, the income from those reading the book through Kindle Unlimited is five times more than those who purchase the book. Not that either is very large right now, but I do find it fascinating. Further, it encourages authors to write to get plenty of pages out there for our readers to enjoy. It seems like a very good 'win-win' scenario to me.

Feel free to jump on the Facebook page to ask me any questions about being an Author on Amazon. I'm happy to share what experiences I can.

I've mentioned before, my writing is more escapist. I love a good action story, but more than that, I want to engage with the characters. I want to feel what they are going through if possible. I want situations that make me get excited, worried, laugh and say, "Take that, sucka!" out loud. The challenges faced by the protagonists don't have to be life-threatening, it could be a challenge to ask that special someone for a date that keeps the story flowing. I'm not really into books that keep you constantly afraid for the characters. If I care about a character, I'll turn the page, and buy the next book, just to see them reach a personal milestone that is challenging to that character. However, having said all that, action is what drives the story forward.

In this story, Bethany Anne shows her fun side a little more. The cussing can be a bit extreme, but she uses it (as do John, Eric, Darryl, and Scott) in a fun way.

There really is a Joe's Famous Hot Dogs & Burgers (in Florida City – https://www.facebook.com/

## AUTHOR NOTES: MICHAEL ANDERLE

JoesFamousHotDogsBurgersMore). There really is (or was) a house for sale in Key Biscayne for $8.9 million with nine bedrooms. I imagine someone will buy it, but in my books, Bethany Anne already has! Joe's Pizza in New York City is already famous, they don't need a shout out from me. :-)

I honestly had *no* plans for Bethany Anne to set up a base in Miami. It will be fun to see what she does with it. Now she has two houses, I can only imagine that John wants to move next door after the close call he had with Ms. Joshwood and Bethany Anne.

There are presently thirteen titles sketched out, and I expect more after that. *Queen Bitch* is the second in the series. The next title is tentatively *Love Lost,* where the enemy decides to attack Bethany Anne indirectly. They find out it is a really good way to piss off a very powerful enemy. Further, Bethany Anne needs to start building her military, scientific, and business infrastructure as she aims for the stars.

To accomplish these goals, she needs good people.

Please, if you enjoyed this book, give it a good rating on Amazon? Your kind words and encouragement help any author. I will continue to the next story whether you provide an *outstanding* review or not. However, it might get done a wee bit faster with the encouragement (smile).

As of today (11/11/2015), nine days since I released the first book, I have two 5-star ratings on *Death Becomes Her*. I've turned around the second book in nine days. Imagine what I could do with fifty 5-star ratings!

Okay, that's not true. I can't write and edit that fast :-(

You can find book links on my Amazon Author Page here:

http://www.amazon.com/Michael-Anderle/e/B017J2WANQ/

Want to comment on the best (scene, comment, event, shoes or gun for Bethany Anne, a weapon Nathan would prefer...you name it) join me on Facebook:

## AUTHOR NOTES: MICHAEL ANDERLE

https://www.facebook.com/TheKurtherianGambitBooks/

Want to know when the next book or major update is ready? Join the email list:

http://lmbpn.com/email/

Thank you,
Michael Anderle, 2015

*All credit for me having *any* shoe knowledge goes to my wife, who still works to provide me with even a finger's amount of fashion sense. Why she asks me to comment on her outfits in the morning still confuses me to this day.

BOOKS BY MICHAEL ANDERLE

For a complete list of books by Michael Anderle, please visit:

**www.lmbpn.com/ma-books/**

## CONNECT WITH THE AUTHOR
### MICHAEL ANDERLE SOCIAL

Website:
http://lmbpn.com

Email List:
http://lmbpn.com/email/

Facebook Here:
https://www.facebook.com/TheKurtherianGambitBooks/

Made in the USA
Columbia, SC
02 May 2022